a novella

by Chuck Hunter

Published by Chuck Hunter

Pain's Joke is a work of fiction. Names, places, and incidents are either products of the author's imagination, or are used fictitiously.

CONNECT WITH CHUCK HUNTER ONLINE!

PainsJoke.com

chuckhunter.blogspot.com

Facebook.com/ChuckHunterAuthor

S.P. - I'm sorry I forgot how awesome you are. Thank you for reminding me.

A.S. - I owe you a beer.

Chapter 1

An early summer breeze playfully wrestled with the leaves of the maples and oaks on Dorn's Hill. But the breeze surrendered its friendly tussle, and it tumbled down the mountainside into the basin below, wherein laid the town of Allardale, Ohio. It was Sunday morning, and a few of the inhabitants of the once-bustling, now sleepy logging town were preparing for church services. Others, enjoying a day off, were sleeping in. Still others had begun mowing the lawn or repairing the awning over the porch. The breeze, careful to keep the Sabbath, didn't bother causing too much trouble. It stirred the warm air with the scent of blooming iris, and it tossed around a candy wrapper dropped by children in the parking lot of the drug store. It nudged an empty foam cup past the pumps of the gas station to the east. The cup rolled to the unkempt patch of weeds between the gas station and a vacant gravel lot then stopped. The breeze pushed a little harder, and the cup flipped a few times and came to rest in a thick patch of milkweed and dandelions growing from the gravel. It was an easy wind; the kind of breeze that carries daydreams to a person as they lay in a hammock between the oaks in the backyard. It was the type of gentle wind that gives a person an extra couple of feet on

their cast when fishing, but only if they cast at just the right time.

The breeze continued down Main Street, through the center of town, past the fire station and the grocery store, and eventually found its way into the kitchen window of Dolores Pike. Already dressed for church in a pastel floral sundress and a "Kiss me, I'm Irish" apron, she was rinsing the leftover egg yolk from the dishes so that it wouldn't cake up when she and her son, Jonas, were gone. Dolores' husband, Paul Jenkins, was still in bed with a hangover. Jonas was sitting on the edge of the couch trying to button the sleeves of his dress shirt. He was a healthy boy in most respects, but a birth defect had caused an excess amount of calcium to be deposited along the side of his jaw, resulting in a very visible protrusion along his left jawline. The condition didn't cause him any physical pain, but with such a disfiguring condition, school yard taunts and stares were inevitable.

"You ready, honey?" Dolores asked as she dried her hands on a dishtowel and swiftly removed her apron, tossing it over the back of the kitchen chair on her way to the living room.

"I'm coming, ma," Jonas said. He was having trouble buttoning a sleeve.

"Oh, Jonas, we're gonna be late," she said, stooping down to help him. "Besides, I wanted to stop and see Momma before church." Dolores always visited her mother's grave before going to church. Jonas felt uncomfortable seeing his mother talk to a headstone, and he always stayed in the car. She offered him her hands to help him off the couch. "C'mon now, baby."

"Ma," he rolled his eyes, "I ain't no baby. I'm twelve and eleven twelfths."

Bending over to kiss his forehead, she said, "I know honey, but you'll always be my baby. Now get out the door and into the car. We're gonna be late."

******

Dolores pulled into the gravel drive which split the cemetery in two. She parked the rusted blue sedan under the largest maple tree. It was actually two maple trees, which grew only inches apart from each other, and the trunks had fused themselves together over the years, resulting in the appearance of one tree with remarkably dense foliage. On sunny days, the shade kept the car from getting too warm for Jonas while he waited. Paul had promised to fix the air conditioning last summer, but he never got around to it. She rolled down Jonas' window to allow the breeze in.

"I won't be long. You just sit tight." she said.

Jonas twitched when the car door shut. He watched his mother walk down the row of headstones and disappear over a small hill.

"All them dead people," he whispered. He closed his eyes and leaned his head back against the seat. He enjoyed the warm breeze coming through his window, and he listened to the birds chirping. In the distance, a lawn mower was buzzing. He was about to fall asleep when he heard the crunch of shoes meeting gravel. The sound was coming toward him. Jonas' pulse increased. He was almost certain it was one of the zombies he had seen in the late-night movies on Channel 3. He slowly opened his eyes, leveled his head and looked into the side mirror. He was relieved to see that it was only an old man walking up the cemetery drive.

Jonas watched through the side mirror until the old man veered off to the right, cutting diagonally between rows of headstones. He leaned his head out of the window to get a better look at the old man. He was wearing black polyester slacks with suspenders, and a white short-sleeved shirt, buttoned to the collar. In his right hand, he carried a plain bamboo cane. At the row near Jonas's window, the old man turned right and continued to walk a few paces to a small, inconspicuous grave. He stood still for a moment before using the cane to help him kneel. He reached down to brush the grass clippings off the flat headstone and again enlisted the help of the cane in standing. Jonas watched as the old man removed a small white handkerchief from his back pocket, blew his nose, and folding it carefully, returned it to his pocket.

"Yuck," Jonas said as his mother opened her car door.
"Yuck what?"

"That old man over there just blew snot into a hanky and put it back into his pocket. Just like that." He mimed stuffing a handkerchief into his pocket.

"What do you suggest people should do with their snot, hon?" she said, laughing.

"I just blow it onto the grass. Paul taught me that."

"Well, Paul ain't like normal folk, dear. You oughta know that by now. And you shouldn't let him teach you bad habits like that."

"I bet that old man's momma hollers at him for putting boogers in his pockets."

She stared at the old man briefly, and then her brow lowered. "No, his momma's on the other side of the cemetery. He's here to see his wife," Dolores said as she started the car. "We're gonna be late if we don't get goin'." Jonas continued to watch the old man as they drove away from the tall maple tree.

Chapter 2

Dolores and Jonas attended the Allardale Pentecostal Assembly. It was a large church for such a small town. The attendance was usually around a hundred people on an average Sunday morning. For Easter or Christmas services, attendance peaked at around one hundred and fifty, but that included all of the relatives of church members and the folks who only came on Easter and Christmas anyway. The church was nestled back in the woods off County Road 12 about a half mile past the "Welcome to Allardale" sign. It was the only Pentecostal church in town, but the congregation frequently planned clothing and canned food drives with the congregations of St. Stephen's Catholic Church and the Weir County Methodist Church.

Dolores led Jonas into the sanctuary through the glass double doors at the back. With her hand on his shoulder, she chose a pew in the back so as not to disturb those who were already worshiping. The congregation was already into the third verse of "The Old Rugged Cross" when Jonas sat down. She remained standing. Jonas attended the adult worship service instead of the children's Sunday School classes. It wasn't so much because he was shy as it was because Dolores was overprotective when it came to his socialization. She knew how hurtful kids could be at his age, and being the best mother she knew how to be, she wanted to keep him from that pain as much as possible.

When the song was over, the congregation took their seats and Pastor Harkness took to the pulpit.

"I'd like to let everyone know, before I get into the sermon, that Sister Hazel Osterman – Sister, raise your hand so everyone can see you – Sister Hazel's having a Candle Party this Tuesday at her house at six thirty. All the ladies of the church are invited, and there'll be samples and giveaways and such. If you need directions, ask Sister Hazel after the service.

"Also, how many of you parents are sending your youngin's to summer camp?" Rev. Harkness asked as he raised his hand and scanned the congregation. "OK, about twenty or so. Well you need to have your child's permission slip signed and returned to our Youth Minister by May 15th. Any later and your kids won't be able to attend.

"Don't forget about the annual church picnic. That'll be on Saturday, May 25th from noon until ten or eleven, depending on when the bonfire goes out, I guess, right Brother Frye? You all can tell by my waistline that I never pass on all that good cooking there." The congregation chuckled. "There'll be barbecue chicken, hot dogs, hamburgers, macaroni salad, potato salad, cole slaw, banana pudding, fruit salad, and ALL kinds of good, good food.

"And I know I said they'd be quick announcements, but lastly, and probably most important to me, at least, is the Father Son Fishing Day at Teeters Lake State Park. That's gonna be the third Saturday in June. We'll all be meeting at the parking lot there by the boat ramp. If you don't have boats , there's probably gonna be three or four boats that are only gonna be about half full, so I'm sure these good brothers would love to share some space. Or, if you're like me, there's some real nice grassy spots to the left of the parking lot where you can set up a chair and fish from the shore."

"Ma, do you think Paul and me can go to that?" Jonas asked.

"Shh, baby, I'll ask him when we get home." she whispered, patting him on the thigh. She and Paul married in February, and she thought the outing would be a great opportunity for "her boys" to get to bond with each other.

The pastor delivered a fiery sermon on the benefits of living a spirit-filled life, interjected hallelujahs and amens from the congregation. One church member, Brother Peterson always gave a loud "Whew!" followed by a, "C'mon brother, preach it!" while he raised his Bible in the air whenever he agreed with what the pastor was saying.

As the sermon was winding down, the pastor gave an invitation to come to the altar and be prayed for if anyone wanted to accept Jesus into their life. When nobody came forward after a minute or two, he dismissed the service with a prayer.

"So can I go fishin' with Paul, Momma?" Jonas asked again as the congregation stood up and gathered their Bibles, purses, and crumpled balls of tissues.

"Now, I told you…I'll ask him when we get home. If he's awake. But I do think it'd be a good idea for you two to get some time together. Just the two of you. Doing something besides blowin' your noses on the lawn." Dolores tapped his behind with her purse.

Chapter 3

When the two of them returned home, Paul was waiting in the living room. Drunk again, he had slouched himself into the recliner and was picking at the label on the beer bottle with his thumb while cursing at the baseball game on television.

"Damnit! You sonsa bitches, that was a strike!" he shouted at the twenty inch screen as if he was expecting a personal reply. Paul quickly raised his fist to scratch his chest and mumbled under his breath, "Damn shitbirds wouldn't know a strike—"

Paul was rough, but handsome. His dark brown eyes were what attracted Dolores to him when they first met at the Food Lion. He came through her register line with a carton of Winston's, a case of Budweiser, and a fishing magazine. He flirted with her while she rang him up, and she blushed. Twenty minutes later, he came back through to purchase an assortment of flowers from the florist inside the store. After she gave him his change and receipt, he gave her the flowers and asked her what time she got off work. They dated for three months when he proposed, and they married two months later, a first marriage for both of them. "I'm gonna go ride my bike, momma," said Jonas before they walked through the front door.

"Okay honey, but change your clothes and be back soon. I'm fixin' to cook lunch." Dolores placed her purse and keys on the kitchen counter and walked back into the living room to kiss Paul on the cheek. "You miss us, babe?"

Paul wrapped his arm around her waist and pulled her into his lap. "Dory, I miss you every time you go off anywhere," he replied with a passionate kiss on her lips, followed by a firm grasp to her behind. "But the view of this as you walk out the door … mmm," he said as he kissed his fingertips in bad impression of a chef.

She playfully slapped his chest. "Oh please, Paul. This big ol' thing?"

"Pfszh! Whatever. Baby that's what keeps me warm at night."

"Oh, so I'm just an electric blanket to you then?" she asked jokingly. "C'mon now, honey, you know I was only kiddin'."

Jonas, now changed into his favorite sweatshirt and jeans, ran through the kitchen, through the living room and out the front door. "Goin' to the park momma!" he yelled as the screen door slammed behind him.

"Be back in an hour, hun." She said while she leaned over to get a better view of him running down the street.

Paul finished his beer. "What's for lunch?"

"Oh, I don't know. Maybe some hamburgers or meatloaf. What would you like?"

"You!" he growled as he nibbled at her neck.

"Paul! Stop being dirty, we just got outta church," she

said playfully as she got up from his lap and straightened her dress. "Speaking of, the men of the church are having a fishing day at the park next month."

"Dory, I go fishing so I don't have to go to church. God made the trees and the fish and water, didn't he?"

"I know, honey, but Jonas was really looking forward to—"

"Forward to what? Making faces and scaring all the fish away?"

Her eyes narrowed, her nostrils flared and she stood up. "How dare you, Paul? You know he can't help how he looks."

"Sorry," he said flippantly. "But I don't want him throwing rocks into the water, and talking the whole damn time."

"Don't talk like that Paul, he ain't a five year old. He's almost a teenager."

"Well I dunno. I might have to work. Is that a Saturday? I'd really rather not go fishing with them Bible thumpers. How do they expect to fish without beer?"

"Just please, Paul? For Jonas?" she asked as she stuck out her bottom lip and gave him her best puppy dog eyes.

"I said lemme see if I have to work," he said, annoyed.

Forgiving him of his earlier remarks, she kissed him on the cheek. "Thank you, sweetie. Besides, I know you guys'll have fun."

Outside, Jonas was crouched under the open living

room window listening to the conversation. He couldn't understand why his mother would marry such a mean man. He dried a small tear with his palm, wiped his nose with the back of his hand, and walked around the back of the house to the shed which housed his bicycle. From the kitchen window, Dolores watched him stomping through the yard, and she knew he had overheard the conversation. She watched as he pedaled down Cambden Street.

Up and down the east side of Cambden Street were an assortment of rundown bungalows and a mix of old and new trailer homes, some on foundations, most simply propped up by cinder blocks. It was the type of neighborhood where only the old people took care of their property, and even then it was by placing reflecting balls on pedestals in their yards. Or those wooden cutouts, painted to look like an old lady bending over the flower bed, exposing her skivvies. On any warm day a person would see filthy dogs chase children on hand-me-down bikes. On the west side of the street were railroad tracks, and running parallel to them was the creek.

The Pike house was at the north end of the street. It was a two bedroom, wood-sided bungalow without central air conditioning; a shotgun shack with a two-course footer, essentially. The white paint had faded overall, and it was beginning to peel near the ground. They didn't have a driveway or a garage. Dolores' sedan and Paul's truck were parked in the gravelly netherworld that exists between the

grass and the blacktop. It was a modest, but tired, house.
Dolores tried her best to decorate it given their budget, and
Paul took depressingly inadequate care of the property. The
roof needed repaired because rain water would leave
concentric brown circles on the ceiling in the corner by the
front wall and the wall separating the living room and
kitchen. Whenever Paul wasn't too busy working or
watching the television, he would attempt a half-assed repair
job around the house. But he certainly wasn't a skilled
tradesman, and the remedy would often look worse than the
problem itself. For instance, every three or four years, the
creek would rise past its banks and flood ten or twelve inches
of their footer. When the waters receded, they left behind a
brownish green mold. Paul would grab a deck brush and a
water hose and begin scrubbing it off. By the time he
worked half way toward the back of the house, he would be
too drunk to stand, and he would leave the job unfinished.

  The patchy, crabgrass yard was surrounded by a rusted
chain link fence, and nobody ever bothered to close the gate.
In the back yard was a maple tree about thirty feet tall. It
was perfect for climbing, but Jonas never ventured past the
lower limbs. He was always afraid of losing his grip and
falling. A homemade doghouse, a remnant from the
previous owner, sat in the far left corner of the back yard.
When Paul bought the human house, Dolores convinced him
to keep the doghouse with the intention of getting a puppy
for Jonas. But with their jobs and financial constraints, a dog

never materialized.

A week ago, Paul received an offer on the house from a developer who was intent on demolishing the entire neighborhood to make way for a modern, lower middle-class development, complete with sidewalks and cul-de-sacs. Paul was determined to hold out for a better deal, so he rejected the offer and never spoke a word about it to Dolores.

About a half mile from the Pike residence was the Larson Avenue bridge, one of only two which connected the halves of the town. Larson Avenue began at County Road 12 on the west side of town by the PVC pipe factory where Paul worked, and it ended at Route 41 on the east side by a used car dealership and a McDonald's. East of Rt. 41, it was just a dirt road heading into the hills.

Jonas usually enjoyed walking down to Taylor Avenue. It was one of the handfuls of streets in the town that had sidewalks, and there was a small park near his school, only a few blocks from the corner of Taylor and Brock. After church on Sundays, he would ride to the park and play by himself until he got hungry and returned home, or until Dolores picked him up. Spurred on by anger about Paul's comments, however, he rode past the park. He continued down Taylor, past the music store and what used to be a men's clothing store. He rode past the ice cream stand, and for no reason other than to wander, turned left onto Main.

As he turned the corner, Jonas noticed the old man

from the cemetery walking toward him. He quickly squeezed his brakes and came to a skidding stop. He turned around and ducked back behind the corner. He leaned his bike against a picnic table between the ice cream stand and the abandoned clothing store. A moment later, the old man rounded the corner and stepped up to the window of the ice cream stand. Placing the handle of his cane in the crook of his right elbow, he removed change from his pocket with his left hand and separated out ninety-five cents with his right index finger. The girl behind the window handed him a small vanilla cone. He tipped his hat, grabbed a few napkins from the holder on the counter and walked toward Jonas.

"Is this seat taken?" he asked. Jonas stared at him for a moment then shook his head. The old man sat down and removed his hat. "Sure is a fine day, idn't it?" Jonas scuffed the toe of his tennis shoe into the pavement. "You're not much of a talker, are you? My boy was shy. Never understood why he'd go off to the Army an' all. With all them folks he don't know, you'd think he'd stay away from that sorta thing."

"I'm not shy. I was just scared. I saw you at the cemetery this morning," said Jonas defensively.

"Oh yeah?"

"Yeah, I thought you was a zombie at first."

"Ha, well if it rests your mind any son, I ain't a zombie. You musta been watchin' that movie last night, huh? I saw that flipping through the channels."

"Yeah. I was waiting for momma to come home from work. She's the one I was with at the cemetery. We go there every week before church."

"I'm there once or twice a week myself. My name's Reverend James Chambers, the second," he said as he stuck out his hand. "Nice to meet you."

"Jonas. Nice to meet you too."

The reverend ate his ice cream and watched traffic go by for a moment. Then he suddenly continued the conversation as if he was compelled to speak. "Yeah, my mother is buried there, and so is my wife. The missus passed about twelve, or was it thirteen? Twelve or thirteen years ago. I go there to see her, keep her up on things, tell her about my day, y'know just talk to her. Sounds crazy doesn't it?"

"Momma does the same thing. She goes and sees my grandma and talks to the headstone. I always thought it was kinda weird."

"Yeah, I suppose I could see how someone would think that's a little crazy. It's not like the dead can hear us or anything. I know she's dead, it's just that I get lonely and I miss her. And if I talk to her, it's almost like I've got her back for a little while. Even if it's a one-sided conversation, it's better than nothing at all."

"Whatever. I still think it's weird."

"A lot of people go to cemeteries and talk to their loved

ones."

"A lot of people steal, but it don't make it right."

"True, true."

"I learned that the hard way. One time, I stole some candy from the Food Lion, and momma liked to have whooped me for it too. Didn't steal again, that's for sure. You ever steal anything?"

"No, son, never have. Some folks think I did. Let me tell you, it's tough being accused of doing something you didn't do."

"What do you mean?"

"Oh it's a long story..."

Jonas looked Rev. Chambers in the eye.

"Okay then, I guess. Where do I begin? Well, there used to be another Pentecostal church in Allardale. I started The Allardale Holiness Church sometime in 1953. It started as a Bible study in our home, and as it grew, we moved into the old storefront near downtown. The Lord blessed us, and we enjoyed great success during the 60's and 70's. The eighties were rough, what with the mill closing and all. But attendance picked back up after that pipe factory went in. And, oh I guess it was around 1998 a slick out-of-towner with a get-rich-quick pyramid scheme came into town and targeted our church. He was promising the sun, moon, and stars, I tell you. He said he was gonna make us all rich. I didn't want to be rich, well I did, but I didn't want to be rich for why you think. I wanted to use the money we'd make and put it back into the church. Pay off the mortgage, start a van ministry, hire a secretary, help other people in town who couldn't pay for groceries and whatnot. Well, he conned me into convincing the congregation into getting in on the plan and in a few months, the out-of-towner was gone, never heard from again. Those who felt as if they had been taken advantage of split ways with our church and started their own church: Allardale Pentecostal Assembly."

"That's where me and momma go," Jonas interrupted.

Rev. Chambers continued. "Well, within a few months, attendance at Allardale Holiness Church dwindled down to a handful of old folks, who would toss a dollar or two into the offering plate when it was passed. Pretty soon, we weren't able to pay the mortgage and the bank foreclosed. By 1999 the doors were closed. My wife, Esther, she was so embarrassed. She couldn't go to anywhere without people saying things behind her back, sometimes right to her face, and sometimes just stare at her with dirty looks. They all blamed me for losing all that money, and I am to blame for getting them all involved. But he had solid paperwork, showing his proven track record for making money. I figured I'd be able to help everyone by getting them all a little something to fix the house with, or buy a new car with. Greed, I suppose, was the overall reason. Anyway, my Esther, she just couldn't take it anymore and... well, she took a handful of sleeping pills before bed one night. She never woke up."

"That's awful."

"Well, you know, you can't really be sure how anything in life is gonna turn out. Not a day goes by without me feeling guilty. I guess the Lord wanted to teach me something. Humility maybe. I don't know anymore."

"You can't really blame yourself."

"Oh, I know, I know. Everybody says that. Everybody who didn't have a thing to do with it will remind you about your role in it. Not on purpose, mind you. But they do. Over time, it just settles on you like a ... well, I don't know what like. I used to have a real good metaphor for just this occasion, but I've kept to myself for the past ten years, and gone and forgot it." The reverend paused for a moment and looked upward. "Heh! Can't remember for the life of me. But anyway, I told myself a while ago that I'm gonna own up to my part in it all. And so now I repay my debt to her by going to see her, telling her that I'm sorry, and giving her flowers and all. I don't know what else I can do."

"Pastor Harkness says that when you're stuck and you don't know what to do that you should pray and ask God to tell you."

Rev. Chambers chuckles. "Son, if it was that easy, I'd a prayed a long time ago. Besides, I ain't a preacher anymore. I don't have a building, don't have a congregation, I'm too old for all that. And honestly, I'm not sure I believe in it all anymore. I'm just living out the rest of my sentence here until

I can pass on, and hopefully get to see her again in person and apologize properly. I tell you what, if I actually do make it to heaven, it'll be a miracle."

"Pastor says to expect miracles to happen when you pray, and they will."

"Is that so? Well, I'll keep that in mind, but don't expect to see my Esther walking around town anytime soon."

"Now you sound like Momma. I don't think she believes in miracles."

"I don't know what I believe anymore, to tell you the truth."

"You two should start a club. The We-Don't-Believe-In-Miracles Club."

"Ha! I suppose so. I'll think about that. Well," the reverend said, wiping the corners of his mouth with a napkin, "It's been nice talking to you. It really has. I haven't really told anyone that whole story before. Strike that- one if you count the cat as a person. It feels kinda good to get it out."

"Like a burp."

"Ha! I guess, son. I reckon I'll be seeing you around."

"See you, pastor," he replied and watched the old man walk away. Just then, he noticed the old man had left his hat. "Hey!" said Jonas as he grabbed the old man's hat. "You forgot this."

"Why thank you, son. Tell you what," he said as he reached into his pocket. "Here, go buy yourself a cone." He handed Jonas a dollar.

"Thanks," said Jonas.

The old man placed the fedora on his head, tipped it, and said, "You're quite welcome, youngin'. You take care now."

Jonas bought his ice cream and ate it as he walked his bike back toward home. A block from home, he crumpled up the leftover napkins and threw them into a trashcan in front of a trailer. He checked his chin in the side mirror of a van parked on the street for any drips of vanilla. He knew Paul would ask all sorts of questions about how he came across the ice cream, and he would probably accuse him of begging if Jonas told the real story. Jonas knew it was best not to arouse any suspicion in Paul, especially after he'd been drinking.

Jonas could smell his mother's meatloaf from the front porch. The sounds of the baseball game on television were roaring through the living room windows. Dolores was in the kitchen, setting the table for herself and Jonas. Paul preferred to eat his meals in front of the television.

"I made meatloaf, baby. With A-1 instead of ketchup, just the way you like it. Go wash up now. After lunch, we're gonna go to the store and rent a movie for tonight."

"While you're out, why don't you pick me up some more beer?" asked Paul, leaning unsteadily in the recliner to remove his wallet from his back pocket.

"Why don't you pace yourself, and maybe you'd have

some beer left at the end of the day?"

Paul glared and threw a twenty at her.

Dinner was relatively silent, and it was only sporadically interrupted by Paul's cursing at the television whenever the umpire made what he determined to be bad calls. Jonas ate his meatloaf and asked for seconds. He ate that and asked for thirds. At the end of his third plate, Dolores looked under the table jokingly to make sure he wasn't throwing it on the floor.

"Well, someone's got an appetite today," she said.

With a mouthful of meatloaf, Jonas replied, "I did a lot of ridin' today. Besides, I'm a growing boy. I need the vitamins and stuff."

"Oh, I bet you do. Chew with your mouth closed, baby." She refilled his glass of milk. "So where'd you go, the park?"

"No. I didn't feel like it, so I just rode around."

Dolores nodded and took another bite of meatloaf.

"Momma, you remember that man from the cemetery?"

"Yeah, honey, why?"

"I saw him. He was at the ice cream stand."

"You weren't talking to strangers were you? I've told you about that. Someone'll come and snatch you up and hurt you."

"No, mom. Gosh. I was just riding around." Jonas felt guilty about lying to his mother. For whatever reason, he felt that it was important to keep that old man to himself. As if the old man was a hidden treasure; Jonas was the explorer who found it. It occurred to Jonas that his mother was still talking to him, and he wasn't paying attention.

"Did you hear what I said, Jonas?" she asked, tapping her fork on his plate.

"Huh?"

"I said, Paul said that he might go to the Fishing Day with you if he doesn't have to work. Wasn't that nice of him? I think after you're done eating, you should go in there and tell him thank you, don't you?"

"Can I be excused?" Jonas' mind was busy trying to remember how kind the old man was to him and forget how cruel Paul was. He pushed away from the table, ran to his room, and shut the door.

"Jonas! Jonas! You're gonna hurt Paul's feelings—"

"Ungrateful bastard. Why the hell should I go fishing with that?" belched Paul from the living room.

"Paul! You're only gonna make things worse. Jonas, baby, I'm gonna go to the store and get that movie. Was there anything you wanted to see?"

Paul leaving, Jonas thought, but he sat on the bed silent.

"Paul, you see if you can talk to him. Maybe he's just at that age, y'know. God, it might even be a girl or something that's bothering him. I'll be back in a bit." She kissed Paul on the cheek and left the house.

Paul stared at the television for a while. Then he looked around the living room. He slowly got up from the recliner. While scratching his chest, he walked into the kitchen and opened the fridge door. He grabbed the last beer from the shelf, belched and shut the fridge door.

"Hey, Jonas." Paul yelled at Jonas' door as he walked toward it. "You having girl problems?" He leaned against the door, slurring, "I'll tell you what. Just take that girl by the hand, tell her she's the purtiest thing you ever seen, and lay a fat one on her. Ha, ha! Just like that. Lemme tell you. And if she don't like it, give her another big smooch. That'll solve your problems."

The only problem I have is you, thought Jonas.

"Or, or, I'll tell you what," he laughed in a drunken stupor, "is she retarded like you? In that case you'll have to take her by her foot. Ha, ha, ha!"

Why can't Momma see how mean you are?

"Open this door, you little retard. Lemme tell you somethin'." He paused and took another swill of beer "Your momma, she's too nice. If you were mine, I'd a beat you by now. Acting all silly over a girl. Girls ain't nothing but trouble, Jonas. You remember that, you little bastard." Turning away from the door, and stumbling back toward the living room, he said, "Do you even know what a bastard is?" He slumped into the recliner and shouted, "It's you! Ha, ha! That's what it is—"

I hate you. I wish Momma would walk back in. Maybe she forgot her keys or something.

"Jonas. Jonas? Aw, to hell with you, little som'bitch. My game's back on." He pointed the remote at the television, shook it, then pointed it again and turned up the volume.

Why didn't Momma marry someone nice like that old man? He wouldn't make fun of me. I bet he'd even take me fishing if I asked. Paul's mean, and he cusses a lot. I wish Momma could see the way he treats me when she ain't around.

Jonas sat on the edge of his bed until Dolores returned from the store. Paul had fallen asleep in the recliner, and the television blared the sounds of whatever game was next through the living room windows and into the street. What had happened while she was gone was just another secret Paul kept from her.

Dolores gently knocked on Jonas' door and slowly leaned into the room. "Honey, you okay? I got Angels in the Outfield, have you seen this one yet?"

"I'm fine, momma. I was just tired from riding' my bike, I guess."

"Well why don't you come in to the living room and after Paul's done watching the game, we'll watch this one together."

"How we supposed to watch it with him snoring?"

"He's just tired, Jonas. He works hard, and he likes to

relax on his days off. Come help me do the dishes and then we'll watch the movie, okay?"

Jonas followed her into the small kitchen. She filled the single compartment sink with hot soapy water while he gathered the plates and silverware from the 50's-style, metal-trimmed kitchen table and from the TV tray/end table next to Paul's recliner. She washed and rinsed, he dried. While they worked, they talked about what they had planned for the upcoming week. Now that school was out Jonas' plans consisted entirely of hanging out in the yard or riding his bike to the park. Dolores was scheduled to work evenings the entire week, except Sunday. She had been working at the Food Lion for a little over twelve years. When she got pregnant with Jonas during her sophomore year, her father wanted her to get an abortion, and when Dolores refused, he left saying he then refused to feed, house, and clothe a bastard. She dropped out of high school and began working full time. She found a one room, economy apartment above the TV repair shop downtown, which left her mother all alone. She didn't make much above minimum wage, but with God, government cheese, and Goodwill, she managed to get by. Twelve years later, she was still only a cashier, she still made barely above minimum wage, and she still managed to just get by.

For twelve years it was only she and Jonas, and she grew to be content with her modest lifestyle. Her father offered no support, and as a matter of fact, they had not spoken since the day he left. Her mother had died of cancer two and a half years ago. Dolores felt determined to prove herself. She wanted to show the world that she was capable of making a life for herself and her baby. As she saw it, she was largely successful. She had a job, an apartment, and a handsome, young son. When she married Paul, and they bought their house, their finances didn't become much more manageable. Paul made almost ten dollars an hour at the pipe factory, but after taxes, union dues, V.F.W. dues (he was veteran of the first Gulf War) and the mortgage, most of his money went to buying beer, fishing equipment, and accessories for his truck. Regardless of their situation, Dolores enjoyed doing even the most menial task like washing the dishes, as long as she and Jonas did it together. It reaffirmed her belief that she had succeeded, that she had made a solid family.

Dolores let Jonas pull the drain plug as she rinsed the soap bubbles off her forearms. They shared Jonas' dishtowel to dry their hands. They sat down on the light brown couch she bought from the Goodwill and watched Angels in the Outfield while Paul snored. Dolores leaned slightly against the front of the arm of the far end of the couch with her legs outstretched, and Jonas laid on his back with his head in her lap. Throughout the movie, Jonas kept being distracted by alternating resentment towards Paul and a dull, throbbing pain in his jaw. He told Dolores of neither.

Chapter 4

The Wednesday morning air was warmer and more humid than what was usual for a day in mid June. The weatherman on Channel 3 had said it would rain overnight, but it hadn't. The coming front was moving slower than expected. The sky was overcast, the wind was picking up, and the leaves of the trees were turned upward, begging God to quench their thirst. It would rain, but not for a few hours.

Jonas woke up before the sun. Paul was filling his thermos with coffee, and Dolores was still in the shower when Jonas shuffled into the kitchen, yawning.

"You better get dressed, boy. You got another doctor's appointment."

Not quite awake yet, Jonas heard him but didn't acknowledge him. He opened the fridge door and briefly stood motionless in his underpants, squinting from the bright light. He scratched his behind and yawned, then half-heartedly removed a gallon of milk from the top shelf and shut the door with his foot. Placing the milk on the table next to the cereal box and empty bowl his mother set for him, he asked, "Why do I gotta go to the doctor's again? I just went on Monday."

"I dunno, ask your mom. I'm running late. Tell her I'll see her when I get home." Paul placed the thermos in the lid of the large, black, plastic lunchbox and latched it. He quickly shoved each arm into his dark blue, short-sleeved shirt. It had a patch with his name on it above the left breast pocket. He snatched the keys from the plaque on the wall above the phone, and he left for work.

Jonas stared into the empty bowl as Paul walked out the front door. He heard him start the truck and rev the engine a few times, and when the loud muffler was far enough down the street that it could no longer be heard, Jonas poured a mountain of Count Chocula into his bowl and drowned it in milk. Jonas' spoon clinked against the bowl when he shoveled a heaping portion of crunchy, sugary, chocolatey goodness into his waiting mouth. A drop of milk fell from his pursed lips as he chewed the cereal in his bulging cheeks like a cow chewing its cud.   After a few minutes of clinking and crunching, Dolores rushed into the kitchen sporting a bathrobe and a terrycloth beehive.

"Morning, baby," she said as she kissed him on top of his head. "You better hurry up with that cereal. I gotta take you to Sellarsville to see Dr. Cunningham." She quickly poured a cup of coffee and rushed back down the hall into the bedroom.

All of the morning commotion meant nothing to Jonas. To him, summertime mornings were carefree times. There were cartoons to watch and trees to climb. Summertime was definitely not meant for appointments, especially doctor's appointments. Nonetheless, he finished his cereal and left the empty bowl, the half-empty cereal box, and the gallon of milk sitting on the table when he walked backed to his bedroom to get dressed.

While dressing, he wondered why he had to return to the doctor's office at the hospital. They took some measurements and x-rays of his jaw when he was there Monday. When Dr. Cunningham asked him whether it was giving him any pain, he replied, "Nope." and left it at that.

The rain finally came while Dolores and Jonas were driving North to Sellarsville. The curves the highway became slick, and Dolores slowed down to fifty five miles per hour instead of the posted sixty five.

"Momma, what's the doctor want to see me for?"

Dolores turned off the radio, leaving the car silent except for the ticks of rain on the roof and the squeal of the wipers against the windshield. "Jonas, the doctor took those measurements of your jaw on Monday, and now he wants to tell us what they all mean."

"Is it gonna go away or does he wanna cut on me?"

"I don't know. We'll have to see what the doctor says, baby."

After a few moments of silence, Jonas asked, "Is it ever gonna be like normal?"

A tear formed in the corners of her eye. She blinked, sniffed, and sighed in order to fight away the tears. "I don't know, baby."

"Cuz in church, pastor talked about Jesus healing a crippled man. Maybe he can heal me, too."

"Stop, Jonas. Just stop, okay?"

"What?"

"Jonas, honey, that story was in the Bible as an example of how we're supposed to have faith. It wasn't meant to... I mean, Jesus may have healed him, but...well, when was the last time you saw anybody walking around Allardale healing people?" She looked over and saw the puzzled look on his face. "Oh, you'll understand when you get older, baby."

She wiped her nose with a tissue from her purse and turned the radio on, and the sound of rain on the windows and Faith Hill filled the silence. Jonas peered through the streaks in the side window at a wet, miserable vulture, wings spread, hopping and pecking at the relatively fresh meat of a doe who had lost a race with a semi truck the night before.

****

At Dr. Cunningham's office, Jonas took a seat in the corner and leafed through the magazines on a table next to him while Dolores signed in at the receptionist window. He found a six month old sports magazine, flopped it open on his lap and began flipping through the pages. Halfway through the magazine he stopped to examine a full page ad for an overpriced razor. A handsome, clean shaven face took up the right side of the page. He slowly ran his fingers over the image. Dolores sat next to him, her purse in her lap, humming along to the piped-in music in the waiting room to rid herself of the nervousness of waiting. After a few moments, Dr. Cunningham appeared through a door to the left of the receptionist window.

"Jonas?" he asked with a smile. He ushered them through the door and down a hall to an examination room toward the back of the building. "Have a seat." He motioned toward two chairs as he clipped an x-ray picture of Jonas into the light board on the wall behind him. "So we took a look at the some of the x-rays of Jonas' jaw from Monday. We used a computer to calculate the distances between specific reference points along the bone to determine how much, if any, his jaw is continuing to protrude." He continued explaining Jonas' situation to her, occasionally pointing to the x-ray with the pen from his breast pocket. "...from everything we can tell, there's only been a change of between .5 and .7 millimeters among all the distances. That's not bad at all. I've heard of much worse cases."

"So is it slowing down?" Dolores asked worried.

"Well, it's not slowing down, but at least it's not growing any more than in the previous few years. And that's a good sign."

"So what do you think of fixing it with surgery? He's kinda concerned about that."

"Well, surgery is an option, but not at this stage. And

most insurance companies won't cover it because they consider it a cosmetic problem. Especially in cases like Jonas' where it's not affecting nerves or blood flow to the teeth or tongue. But what we can do for now, and what I think is the best option for the time being, considering that it's not causing him any pain, is I'll give you another script for the drug that slows the calcification, and I'm going to have the ladies up front schedule you for a visit with a specialist in Cleveland. They have a group of orthopedic doctors up there that specializes in facial orthopedic anomalies, and they would be able to give you a lot more treatment options and more extensive knowledge in this specific area. You can call them and work out whatever arrangements would best suit your schedules, and they'll take good care of you." He patted Jonas on the shoulder. "I've seen the folks up there do some really great work with patients like you, Jonas." He shook Dolores' hand and ushered them back down the hall and into the waiting room. "If you have any questions, please feel free to give us a call here."

All Dolores could think about was the scheduling. She would have to take off work in order to take Jonas to his appointments. She thought about picking up a double shift on Wednesdays to free up Thursday, since that was her shortest shift of the week.

When they got home, Jonas turned on the TV in the

living room, and plopped himself onto the couch.　Dolores was worried, however, and walked directly to her bedroom. She thought of having to adjust her work schedule, and what if they did decide to operate?　Her thoughts soon progressed to how different things would be if she hadn't gotten pregnant in the first place.　Memories of the night Jonas was conceived came flooding back.　She fell to her side and curled into the fetal position on the bed.　She had tried desperately for years to kill the memories of that night, but regardless of her tears, her anger or her prayers, the pain haunted her.　The roar of the crowd from the television carried her back to that night.

Chapter 5

"Touchdown! Allardale Wolverines!" yelled the voice over the loudspeakers. "Number 86, Lane Sherman!"

Dolores and Sandy were returning from the concession stand, and they held their popcorns and sodas in the air and cheered.

"He's awesome this year!" Sandy said.

"Awesomely hot." Dolores added, and they both giggled.

"So why don't you go talk to him?"

Dolores blushed. "No, I can't."

"C'mon," Sandy nudged her with her elbow. "You never know. Besides, how do you know his teeth aren't all crooked or something? You gotta get up close."

"Sandy, shut up!" Dolores said through her teeth. "There he is!"

He removed his helmet as he jogged toward the bench. He grabbed a plastic bottle from the water boy and squirted most of it into his mouth. When he leveled his head, he noticed Dolores and Sandy walking along the fence which separated the stands from the field.

"Hey, Dolores!" He shouted as he hopped over an open space between players on the bench, and jogged to the fence, smiling and panting.

"I'll go warm your seat," Sandy said.

The look on Dolores's face screamed, "No! Don't Leave!" but she cleared her throat, put a smile on her face, and turned toward Lane. "Y'know, if you keep that up, you'll be in the pros."

"Thanks. Listen, I don't want Coach catching me over here. I gotta get back in the game. But there's a party tonight after the game over at Skeeter's. I'll give you a ride if you wanna."

"I dunno. Mom's pretty weird about me goin' places and all. It's taken me three years just to be able to come to a football game."

"Sherman! You're in," barked the coach from a distance.

"I gotta go. Meet me at the ticket booth after the game." And with that he slapped his helmet on over his blond hair, winked, and ran back to the field.

Dolores hurried back to her seat in the bleachers. She couldn't help but grin.

"Well?" Sandy asked.

"He asked me out."

"Nuh-uh!"

"Yes! He totally just asked me out to a party tonight!"

"I'm so happy for you!" She hugged Dolores and shrieked.

"So should I go?"

Sandy broke the hug and grabbed Dolores by her shoulders, "Should you go? Are you insane? Yes! Of course, you should go. Why not?"

"Well, you know how my momma gets. She'd never let me go on a date."

"So tell her you're spending the night at my house."

Dolores thought it over, but her excitement won over her obedience. She was invited to a party... by Lane. She first saw him at a pep rally in the gym her freshman year. He was gorgeous; tall and muscular, but thin like any other wide receiver. His blonde hair slouched across his forehead like a movie star caught off-guard, and his penetrating blue eyes captivated her. She was hopelessly infatuated since that day, and by asking her to the biggest party of the year, it made her feel like Cinderella. She continued watching the game with nervous anticipation.

After the game, Dolores waited by the ticket booth as patiently as possible for Lane to shower and change into street clothes. He came walking across the field carrying his shoulder pads over his helmet. She thought he looked like a soldier coming home from war.

"You ready?" he asked as they began walking toward his rusty blue pickup.

"Yeah, well...it's just that I probably need to call my mom and tell her I'm going over to Sandy's house."

"Oh, lying to the folks, eh? Pretty sneaky. Didn't know you had it in you."

Dolores blushed. "No... well, yes. But they're just

really strict, y'know?"

"Yeah, mine are too. But you can call her from my house. I have to stop by and get a jacket. Skeeter's having a bonfire and all, but it feels like it's gonna drop off cold tonight," he said as he opened the truck door for her. He tossed his pads in the bed of the truck and walked around the back of the truck to his door.

"Tell her you're just having fun, y'know? It's not like we're gonna be killin' people or worshippin' the devil. It's just a bonfire." He shut his door and turned the key, which had been in the ignition since he bought it in April from Old Man Wiley's widow. The ignition clicked, the engine turned over, then roared, and finally settled down to a sputtering growl. The radio was playing a slow country love song. Lane smiled and winked at her as he pulled the gearshift down into drive, and they drove toward Pine Hollow where Skeeter's parents owned a hunting cabin.

It wasn't until they were a mile or two out of town before Dolores began wondering how far they were from Lane's house.

"I thought you lived up on the hill by the diner," she asked, not wanting to make him think she was some sort of goody two-shoes for wanting to call her mom. She didn't want to upset Lane either.

He reached under the seat for a metal flask, unscrewed the cap and took a swig. "Oh, I figured I could just wear my flannel shirt in back of the seat there. You can probably use the phone at Skeeter's place," he said. He could tell she was still a little worried. "If you want, I can find a payphone or somethin' but we'd have to go all the way back into town, and I don't want to show up after all the beer's gone."

She figured her mom wouldn't mind if she was only a little late coming home. She would just tell her the game went into overtime.

The ride out of town was peppered with small talk. Lane told her of the time he and Skeeter had gotten arrested for stealing a goat from the old man who lived by the sawmill. They were planning to tie the poor thing to the flag pole in the school's front yard. A police officer happened to have been driving past when Skeeter's 4x4 came tearing onto the school's yard, coming to a complete stop only after knocking the flagpole over. In a drunken stupor, they both had neglected to tie the other end of the rope to the roll bars in the bed, so somewhere between the sawmill and the school, the old man's goat was limping around after having jumped out of the bed of the truck. The officer arrested them both, but on account of the league championship game being on the line, Lane being the best wide receiver in the state, and the fact that Skeeter's father is the Chief of Police, they were let go with a warning. It wasn't until after winning the league championship that Skeeter's father made them collect trash for the Sanitation Department to pay for a new flagpole.

Dolores was excited by Lane. He was handsome. He was popular. He was dangerous. He was everything her father wasn't, and that is what turned her on the most. A sudden urge to rebel had been sparked deep inside her previously pious and proper will. She remembered speeches by her father about squelching the spark of temptation before it became an inferno of sin, but the hairs on the back of her neck and the feeling in her gut told her that tonight was the night. She was going to kiss him.

She wanted to test him to see if he was interested. She unbuckled her seat belt to scoot closer to him, and to her pleasure, he placed his strong, warm arm around her shoulder. Her heart raced as she smelled the mixed scents of fabric softener from his t-shirt and aftershave from his face. Tonight was definitely the night.

Lane pulled the truck into a gravel drive off to the right of the road. The gravel quickly disappeared, and branches began scraping the mirrors of the old, rusty pickup. The dirt road was bumpy, and Dolores had to grab hold of his leg a few times just to maintain her bearings while the truck rocked side to side. Not that she minded. The warm denim (and the strong thigh beneath it) felt good. She had never touched a boy in such a way before. She hadn't even been kissed.

The dirt path curved sharply to the left and up a small, but steep, hill before widening into the clearing where the bonfire was. Twelve or fifteen other cars and trucks were parked along the perimeter of the clearing, and a few more had parked behind the hunting cabin, which Skeeter usually keeps locked. He passed out copies of the key to all the guys on the team so that they could bring their girlfriends out to the woods for a little bit of privacy, provided Skeeter himself wasn't using it.

Lane drove behind the cabin and squeezed the truck between Skeeter's truck and a propane tank which hadn't been used since before Skeeter's dad inherited the land a few years earlier. Dolores crawled out of Lane's door and walked beside him toward the bonfire. Someone had brought their home stereo and ran an extension cord from the cabin to the roof of a car nearby. The music was louder than Dolores had ever heard in church.

"Touchdown! Lane Sherman!" screamed Skeeter as he approached the couple with two beer bottles in the air, mimicking a referee.

Lane grabbed one of the beers from him and slapped Skeeter's enormous gut with the other hand. "What's goin' on, man?"

"Havin' a fuckin' party, brother! Woooo!" Skeeter belched and tossed back his sixth or seventh beer. He chugged most of it, allowing a good portion to spill from the sides of his mouth onto his chest, drenching the jersey he was still wearing. He wiped his mouth with the sleeve of his jersey and gave another belch. "Hey, Dory."

"Hey, Skeeter."

"Dory, ah'm traaashed. I've had, like twenny or thirty, but there's more beer in the fridge in the..the, uh, belch… the cabin."

"Keep it up, man. You earned it," said Lane as he grabbed Dolores' hand and walked toward the cabin. "He's usually got a couple of wine coolers in here for the girls. You want one?"

"Sure…" She hesitated. "I won't get drunk off it, will I?"

"Nah." Lane laughed as he opened the door and walked inside. "Here." He reached into the back of the fridge and pulled out a bottle of something pinkish.

She had never had a drop of alcohol, and her parents were strictly dry. She put the bottle to her lips and sipped a bit of it. It was fruity, and she liked it... a lot. "This is good. I've never had this kind." She said looking at the bottle.

"Really? It's alright, I guess." Lane said, holding up his beer. "But I prefer a good old fashioned American beer."

"I don't really drink all that much," she lied.

"Well me and Skeeter are usually out here with the guys after every game. Even when the season's over, we're out here on the weekends. It's nice out here. Quiet, no neighbors calling' the cops."

"Well that shouldn't really be problem anyway, right?"

He stepped closer to her. "No, we get into trouble and all when we get caught, but I'd rather not pick up trash on the weekends. That shit sucks. I'd rather spend my time with a beautiful girl like you," he said as he reached toward her forehead to brush a stray lock out of her face and tuck it behind her ear.

"Lane," she blushed, "you say that to all the girls, don't you?"

"You like herein' it, don't ya?" he laughed.

"It is nice to hear."

It wasn't long before she finished the wine cooler, and Lane walked over to the fridge to get her another. With his right hand, he pulled out a wine cooler for her and another beer for himself. He tilted his head back, and with his left hand, tilted the already open beer into the sky to finish it off. He tossed the empty into the corner and twisted off the cap for her.

"So did you hear about me going to play for Brighton University next year?"

"Nuh-uh, really? That's so cool."

"Yep, four year scholarship and all. It's gonna be cool. They won the conference championships last three years running."

"You'll be awesome there. You'll probably have all the girls asking for your autograph and stuff."

"Nah... well maybe. No, I'm just kiddin'. You wanna be the first to get my autograph?"

"Sure, but I ain't got nothin' to sign on. You got any

paper?"

He looked at her breasts through her thin knit top. "Well then I'll just have to sign your boobs."

She nudges his shoulder. "Oh, stop!"

"No, but seriously, you ever got anyone's autograph before?"

"No, I never met anyone famous."

"So if I gave you my autograph, I'd be your first?"

"Yep. First."

"So...what you're saying is, you want me to be your first?"

"Stop being dirty, you perv." She laughed.

"I can't help it, Dolores. You're so pretty, and I like you... a lot."

"Well, I like you a lot too."

As the conversation continued, Lane worked feverishly to fit in more innuendo, and Dolores playfully dismissed each one. By the time she was halfway through her fourth bottle, she remembered what she was there to do.

"Tell me somethin'. You wouldn't take advantage of a drunk girl, would you?" Dolores laughed as she leaned in toward his chest.

He wrapped his arms around her shoulders and pulled her in. "Why don't we go to the other room?" he whispered into her ear. She pulled her face out of his chest and blinked two or three times. "It's more private," he began to say, but she interrupted him with a misplaced kiss. It landed squarely on his chin, and she laughed out of nervous embarrassment. "Was this what you were trying to do?" He asked her, and leaned in to kiss her.

They kissed passionately as he walked her backward toward the bedroom. The darkness enveloped them as they passed through the doorway, and Lane nudged the door closed with his foot. The two stood in the dark, musty room kissing and groping at each others' clothes for a few minutes. Dolores had never felt so alive. His warm, soft lips felt like a zap from a 9 volt battery which traveled from her lips to her neck and down her spine. She could feel his strong arms and chiseled abs through his shirt. Her belly felt another jolt of electricity as she felt his warm hand fumbling blindly up her shirt. She gently moved his hands down, but continued kissing him, and within a few seconds she could again feel his large, warm hands against her belly and waist.

He stopped kissing her only for as long as it took him to quickly yank his shirt off from over his head. Dolores slowly raised her hand to his cheek and leaned in to kiss him. She ran her hand down the side of his neck and onto his chest, then his abs. Her heart was racing. She giggled and wrapped her arms around her waist, grabbed the hem of her shirt and lifted it over her head. With every touch, every caress, every kiss, these new sensations were starting to make her feel light-headed. The alcohol only intensified the effect, and soon Dolores started feeling sick. She was dizzy, and the smell of mildew was beginning to push the wine cooler up from her stomach. She fought it back down as they frantically began groping each other. As his right hand slid under the elastic waistband of her panties, she felt her stomach squeeze. At once, her mouth opened wide and a column of pink vomit spewed from her open mouth and splattered Lane's chest. He stood motionless, shocked as he watched her heave again. Dolores wasn't concerned with how embarrassing that moment was, she only wanted the heaving to end.

Lane stepped backward, snatched his t-shirt from the floor behind him and wiped off his chest. He began looking for his flannel shirt while Dolores heaved again, then fell to her hands and knees. He pulled his pants up from around his ankles and buttoned them, then he opened the door and stormed out, leaving the door open. She continued heaving until the last drop of pink, bubbly wine formed a puddle engulfing her hands, and she heaved unsuccessfully a few more times. She spit, wiped her mouth with the back of her hand and slumped over onto her side. The room kept spinning as she panted. She closed her eyes, listening to the sound of her heart pounding.

She opened her eyes when she felt something warm and wet on her face. Skeeter was standing over her head, urinating on her and singing "Rain Drops Keep Falling on My Head". Dolores panicked and tried screaming, but her mouth was covered by duct tape, and her hands were bound behind her back. From between her stinging eyelids she saw the silhouettes of Ted Belamy and Tommy Jacobs, two other football players, walking toward her from between a pair of headlights.

"She's up, man," yelled Tommy over his shoulder.

Dolores realized she was no longer in the hunting cabin. In fact, she was lying on her back, and she was naked... on the ground... in the woods... far from any place she immediately recognized. Shame, embarrassment, horror, and fear flooded her mind. Another silhouette came toward her from the headlights.

"Yeah, she's up," It was Lane.

The faces of Ted, Tommy and Skeeter were joined by Lane in a circle around her. She began kicking at them and screaming, but the duct tape only allowed the remnants of vomit in her mouth to come sputtering out of her nose. Tears started streaming across her cheek and pooled in her ears. They're going to kill me, she thought.

"You gonna puke again?" laughed Tommy.

"No," said Lane with a smirk, "I think she knows better now."

Skeeter stepped on the end of her pony tail to keep her head on the ground, while Lane unbuckled his pants. "Go grab the rest of the beer out of the truck, guys. We're gon' be a while."

Dolores clenched her eyes and uselessly tried to squirm

her way free.

"Ooh! Feisty," Lane laughed as he pried her knees apart. "You keep fightin' and it's only gonna make it worse… ask whats-her-name. What was her name, Skeeter?"

Tommy handed Skeeter another cold one. He cracked it open and said, "Uh, which one? Ha ha ha!"

Stacy…Stacy somethin' er other. Hell, I don't know. She was a fighter, though, wudn't she." Skeeter said as if he were reminiscing about an old football victory.

Dolores struggled hopelessly. Her heart and head were pounding; her muscles were aching from the cold and the exhaustion. Her gaze raced from the faces of each of the boys, to the rotten tree stump beside her, to the headlights of Skeeter's truck, to the almost-full moon peeking through the autumn leaves. She could smell the piss and the beer, the vomit and the dirt. She felt the cold, damp leaves beneath her. Each and every facet of that moment was being permanently etched into her memory. The boys could smell her fear, and it fueled them.

"Guys," Lane motioned to Tommy and Ted, "hold her head still and her eyes open. I want her to watch me." He spit into his hand, and a streaking, searing pain coursed into her with a thrust of his hips. She just wanted it to end. But Skeeter was next, then Ted, then Tommy. She tried screaming, she tried kicking, she tried freeing her hands, but each attempt to get them to stop only resulted in more piss or beer in her face.

They stopped only after she quit fighting them, and when they were done, they stripped off the duct tape and tossed her clothes on the ground beside her.

"Get dressed, bitch!" laughed Ted as he threw a cigarette butt at her. A cloud of smoke billowed from his nose as he exhaled. "And don't think you can go telling anybody about this. You think Skeeter's dad is gonna take your word over his?"

It was still several hours before daybreak. After Dolores dressed, she crawled to the rotten stump beside her and waited for them to leave. She curled her knees to her chest, buried her face into them and convulsed as she cried. She couldn't understand why they had done what they did. She felt guilty about not letting her mother know where she had gone. She thought of how disappointed her mother would be if she found out. She went through a million alternate scenarios in her mind, but thinking of what she could have done didn't take away the pain of what they actually did.

When the boys were done with their beers, they told her to hop in the truck. "C'mon. You can't walk home, we're out in B.F.E," said Skeeter. She was reluctant, but she had no other way home, and so she crawled feebly into the bed of the truck.

Ted pushed her off the tailgate when they had stopped

in the parking lot of the drug store. She could barely stand from the pain, and she needed to vomit more, but she didn't move until the sound of Skeeter's truck was out of range of her hearing. Then she slowly began limping home, embarrassed and broken, and wreaking of urine and vomit, beer and dirt.

Chapter 6

The late morning was overcast, but the weatherman said the sky would clear in the afternoon. Jonas was walking down Main Street toward the playground near the school. A block ago, he had found a broken branch from a maple tree and stripped the twigs and leaves from it. As he walked along, he tapped the stick against the sidewalk to keep a rhythm. He didn't have any particular song in mind, just a familiar beat that kept him at a steady pace as he walked to the playground. Dolores had given him permission to go to the playground and said that she would pick him up at 3:00 pm when she was off.

Jonas stopped in front of the guitar shop because he saw an empty cigarette pack lying on the ground. He stood in front of it and balanced his weight between his feet by shaking his hips side to side. He held the stick like a golf club, slowly drawing it back and swinging. "Fore!" he called out to the surprise of Reverend Chambers, who was walking toward him.

"Easy there, fella," said the old man as the cigarette pack flew past his knee.

"Oh, sorry," said Jonas.

"Heh. Well, that ain't too bad a shot you got there. Where you headed?"

"The park near the school."

"Oh yeah? Mind if I join you? I'm just out for my daily walk."

"I guess," Jonas said and resumed tapping the sidewalk with his stick.

"They say it's supposed to clear up, but I don't know," the old man looked up skeptically at the thin gray clouds. "Who knows? Maybe it will be pretty nice later."

"Yeah," Jonas replied warily.

"You know, I never caught your last name," Rev. Chambers said.

"Pike. Jonas Pike," he replied.

The reverend thought for a moment as they continued their stroll. "I used to know some Pikes here in town. They used to go the church I used to pastor a long time ago. What were their names?"

"Me and mom go to the Allardale Pentecostal Assembly out there by the edge of town."

"Oh, I know that place," Reverend Chambers said, forgetting he had told Jonas the entire story earlier. "It's a good church, good people there."

"I like it, I guess. Ain't never been nowhere else to compare it, though."

"I'll tell you, any church is better than going to no church. I mean me and the good Lord got our issues to work out and all, but – wait a minute. Y'know, I think I know your momma. Is her name Dolores?"

Jonas looked up at him, squinting in the glare of the

sunlight. "Yes, sir. Dolores Pike. She's about as tall as you, with brown hair."

"Oh, definitely. I knew her back when she was still in school. Your grandpa and grandma and your momma used to go to the church I pastored. Good folks, they are. How are they doing?"

"Grandma died a couple years ago. I never met Grandpa. Momma says when she had me, Grandpa moved to Florida. Ain't heard from him since."

"Well I'm sorry to hear that, son. And your momma? She doing OK?"

"I guess. She's always workin'."

"Oh. So, you just wander the streets all day? Your momma don't mind?"

"Nah, she said I could go to the park. She's gonna pick me up there at three if you wanna say hi."

"Oh, I don't think I can stay that long. I have some errands to run, and the cat is gonna need let out. I gotta finish my morning walk if I expect to get it all done today. I'm gonna get goin' Jonas. But if you could tell her I said hello, I'd appreciate it. Your momma's a good woman. You better be listenin' to her."

"I will, take care," Jonas replied. He watched Rev. Chambers walk a few steps, then he commenced tapping the stick against the cement, then a storefront step, a parking meter, a lamppost, and a trash can as he continued toward the park.

The sun was starting to peek through the low hanging clouds, and as Jonas reached the park, he took off his sweatshirt and hung it over the back of a park bench near the swings. He always avoided the slide and the monkey bars, deeming himself too mature. The swings, however, were all his. He loved the rush of the wind on his face as he swung. As the swing approached its most forward position and temporarily stopped before retreating towards the rear, his stomach felt light and his skin tingled. He felt as if he were floating above the town. Sometimes he would imagine that he could just keep going up, the swing left rider less behind him as he soared high above Allardale. With each swing back, he would close his eyes and prepare for the swoop forward. Back and forth, back and forth, his legs would fold and extend with a steady rhythm. Jonas swung for hours, entirely consumed by his daydreams of flying.

A few kids came to the playground throughout the day. Some had their parents in tow; other kids around Jonas' age came by in groups of three or four. Even a group of three teenagers came by to smoke a joint in the tree line. All of them eventually left, but Jonas remained. By three o'clock, Jonas had pretended to fly all around Allardale and all parts of Weir County. His flight came to an abrupt end with a honk from Dolores' blue sedan.

"Jonas," she shouted out the window. "C'mon baby, it's time for dinner."

Jonas lowered his toes on the back swing and a cloud of dust shot out from the fronts of his shoes. The swing began its forward motion, and he again lowered his feet and dragged them along the dirt gully directly underneath the swing where dark, musty mulch had once been. He finally stopped the swing, grabbed his sweatshirt from the bench and ran toward the car.

"Hey, ma," he said as he shut the car door.

"Hey, sweetie. How was your day?"

He kissed her on the cheek. "It was good. I met that old man from the graveyard today."

"What old man?"

"Remember? The one I thought was a zombie?"

She frowned. "Yeah, well, you be careful hon, not everybody is a nice person..."

"I know, momma, but he knows you. He said you and grandma and grandpa used to go to his church before I was born."

She paused and turned to look squarely at Jonas. "Now, I'm only gonna say this once, and I want you to listen to me, Jonas. You stay away from that man. He's a thief and a liar, and you got no business talking to people who steal and lie. Y'understand?" She stared at Jonas, who stared back at her from the passenger seat perplexed.

"Yes, ma'am," he moaned as lowered his head. "But he seemed really nice. He said good things about you and grandma."

"Jonas, I don't care if he said we were the smartest, prettiest people in the world. You just stay away from him." She gave him one last stern look, put the car into drive, and drove off from the playground.

Once home, Dolores walked to the edge of the kitchen table, and with a half leaning, half squatting motion, she placed two grocery bags onto it. Jonas was carrying the keys and her purse, which he placed on the kitchen counter next to the fridge.

"Go get washed up, and I'll let you help with the chicken." She couldn't stop thinking about Rev. Chambers. What did he want with Jonas anyway? She knew he probably didn't mean any harm and was just being polite, but it didn't change the hate she had for him. In Dolores' eyes, the good reverend was still just a liar and a thief. And she certainly didn't appreciate him talking to Jonas.

Chapter 7

A few weeks had passed, and the days were growing longer. The sun had risen above the horizon but was still obscured through the trees on the eastern shore of Teeter's Lake. It had been sunny and warm for two weeks, and the warm lake released a thin fog into the low lying portions of ground around the public boat ramp. The boys and men of the church were scattered throughout the parking lot, some re-spooling their fishing reels, others finishing their coffee. Most of the boys were at the water's edge throwing rocks and sticks into the water and bragging about the fish they were planning on catching that day. Some of the men who didn't own boats were joining with those who did, and others were setting up their folding chairs in the grassy areas along the shore.

Paul pulled his truck into an empty space, turned off the engine and turned to Jonas. "Boy, I don't want any trouble outta you, y'hear? I mean it. You sit and fish, that's it. If you gotta piss you go piss, but otherwise, keep your trap shut and just fish. I don't get many days off, and the last thing I wanted to do was to come fishin' with a bunch of holy rollers. So mind your p's and q's, keep quiet, and fish, and when we get home, you're gonna tell your mom we had a grand ol' time. Got it?"

"Got it."

They both exited the truck, and Jonas stood at the tailgate while Paul lowered it.

Paul handed Jonas a rod and reel and a pocket sized, clear, plastic tackle box with only a few hooks and bobbers in it. Paul grabbed his own rod, reel, and tackle, and together they walked toward the grassy area at the end of the parking lot opposite of the ramp where Rev. Harkness had already staked out a spot along the shore.

"Well, hello there, Jonas!" Rev. Harkness waved. "And you must be Paul. Nice to meet ya." The reverend extended his hand.

"Lemme put this stuff down here," said Paul. He placed his gear on the grass and shook the pastor's hand. "Yeah, I figured I'd bring Jonas on down here and maybe catch us some fish." Turning to Jonas, he said, "Put the stuff down there next to mine, and go back to the truck for the lawn chairs."

"So how's work going for ya?" Rev. Harkness asked.

Oh god, he wants to talk. "Oh, not bad. It's work. And you?"

"Good, good. But I tell you, we had a problem last week during the service."

Paul stared at him blankly.

"The problem was, you weren't there. Ha ha!" The pastor stopped reeling in his line in order to slap his thigh.

"Yeah, well, y'know work gets all crazy, workin' a lot of overtime, and I just can't seem to wake up in time."

"Oh, I'm just kiddin' ya, Paul. We're happy you and Jonas could make it out here today. I tell ya, all the boys in the church just have a ball out here. And the dads get to spend some quality time with 'em. Can't beat it, brother. You want a Coke? There are some in the cooler on the other side of me here."

"Oh, that's alright. I brought a cooler in the truck. It's probably too heavy for the boy; I better go help him," said Paul. He was really just looking for an out from the conversation with Rev. Harkness. Damn jabber jaws is gonna ruin the whole day, he thought as he walked toward the truck.

At the truck, he told Jonas to set up the lawn chairs a little further from Rev. Harkness. "All his yackin' is gonna scare the fish away."

Paul waited for Jonas to walk away, then he opened the cooler, pulled out a can of Coke, pulled the tab back, and set it on the floor of the bed. He then opened the toolbox next to the cooler, discreetly removed a metal flask, took a few large swills, and chased it with the Coke.

All of the boats were in the water, and the shore anglers were spread out along the water's edge. Returning from the truck, Paul sat in the lawn chair next to Jonas.

"Alright," he said while picking up his rod and reel, "let's see if we can't catch us some fishes." He released the hook from the line guide nearest the reel. Setting the handle of the rod on the ground to his left side, he pulled a few feet of line off the reel with his right hand and held the hook in front of him. He pulled a nightcrawler from the Styrofoam container and shook the dirt off, then with one smooth motion, he fed the worm onto the hook. Paul attached a large bobber about eighteen inches above the hook, and a squeezed two sixteenth ounce lead sinkers onto the line about an inch above the hook. He picked up the rod by the handle, pressed the bale release, drew the pole back, and with a flick of his wrist, he set the tackle to flight. The line whizzed off the reel, and the bobber followed a high arc through the air before it splashed down and eventually came to rest with concentric rings of ripples emanating from it. He gave the reel a turn and listened for the click of the bale engaging while he took in some slack from the line. Then he sat the pole on the ground beside him and settled into the lawn chair for a relaxing day of fishing. Jonas was still struggling with getting the worm onto the hook.

Paul sighed heavily, "Ugh! What's your problem, boy?"

"The worm won't hold still."

"Would you? If someone was trying to stick a big metal hook in ya, would you just sit there and take it?"

"No." Jonas hated when Paul lectured him.

"Well okay then. Just grab hold of him and run it through."

Jonas did as Paul instructed and cast the bait into the water about twenty feet from the shore and close to Paul's bobber.

"There you go. Now just relax, and enjoy a day of fishin'."

Jonas sat in the lawn chair and stared at his bobber for what seemed to him like hours. Within a few minutes, the boaters had all found their "honey holes" and turned off their engines to avoid scaring the fish. In the still of the morning, Jonas heard a woodpecker knocking on a maple tree across the lake.

"You think woodpeckers get headaches?" Jonas asked.

Paul quickly shushed him. Jonas turned his gaze back toward his bobber and waited. For the next twenty minutes Jonas shifted between watching his bobber and watching Paul chain-smoke. He kept his Winston's in the breast pocket of his t-shirt, and when he finished one he would light a new cigarette with the butt of the old one. Every time Paul lit a new cigarette, he would flick the old one into the lake. Rev. Harkness saw this out of the corner of his eye, and he would frown at Paul, but he remained silent.

"Should I cast it somewhere else? I don't think there's any fish right there," said Jonas. "I think we should move our chairs over there." He pointed.

"Damnit, Jonas, you gotta be patient." Paul said with disdain.

"But I wanna catch a fish."

Paul took off his sunglasses and looked sternly at Jonas.

"Boy, you sure do forget fast. I told you in the truck you gotta sit here, shut up, and fish. Now if you don't wanna listen to me, I'll take your ass home."

"But I don't wanna leave! I wanna catch fish!" Jonas insisted.

"I swear to God, I'm leaving now!" Paul shorted. "C'mon, get your shit together and get in the truck."

Jonas wanted to cry, but he held it in. Rev. Harkness heard Paul and spoke up. "Well if you're going to leave, Jonas can stay here with me. I'll take him home when we're done. He'll be just fine."

Paul continued reeling in his line and gathering his gear. "You do what you want, preacher man. I'm leavin'." He turned to Jonas and pointed his finger in his face. "And you can bet I'm gonna tell your momma about this."

Paul stomped off toward the truck with a rod and tackle box under one arm and a lawn chair in the other. He threw his gear into the bed of the truck, jumped in the cab, started it, and pushed the pedal to the floor. A cloud of dirt and a thousand "tinks" of gravel hitting the underside of his truck were all they could see or hear of Paul.

Jonas slowly moved his chair over toward Rev. Harkness.

"Listen, forget about him. He's just being a jerk. Are you okay?"

"I'm alright, I guess." Jonas replied. "He's like that all the time. Except when he's sleeping. Even then he just looks mean."

"Well, it'll be alright. He'll get down the road and cool off some. You'll see." Rev. Harkness consoled him. Changing the subject he asked Jonas, "So where do you think all the fish are? I haven't gotten a bite this whole time."

"I dunno. Maybe over there." Jonas said, pointing to a patch of water lilies. "Bass like to hide under the lily pads and wait for smaller fish to go swimming by. Then they just jump out and eat 'em."

"Sounds like a plan to me. Need some help casting over there? If you get hung up in those lilies, you'll lose your worm."

"No, I can do it," Jonas said as he awkwardly cast his line toward the lilies. The cast was short, and the bobber splashed down fifteen feet in front of his intended target. "Right there," he said as he took in the slack.

"It's as good a place as any, I suppose," chuckled Rev. Harkness.

"Yep," agreed Jonas, before catching a glimpse of the bobber dipping under the surface of the water. It dipped under again.

"You got a bite!" said the reverend excitedly.

Jonas quickly pulled the tip of the rod backward to set the hook, and he began struggling to reel in the catch. "It's a fighter!" he said.

"Ease out on the drag, or he'll snap the line when he runs. That's it! Keep reeling it in!"

Every few seconds the fish would change course and try to escape, causing the line to pull from the reel with a buzzing sound.

"Let him run. Let him run!" Rev. Harness said. "Looks like a bass, fighting' like that. They'll wear out and eventually let you bring 'em in. Lemme grab the net!"

Jonas fought for a few more moments before finally bringing the fish into range of Rev. Harkness' landing net. It was a largemouth bass, and a large one at that.

The reverend extended the net under the fish, while Jonas tried his best to keep the tip of the pole as high as he could. The reverend reached into the net and grabbed the fish by the lower jaw. He lifted the bass out of the net and Jonas got a good look at his catch.

"How big is it?" Jonas asked.

"Oh..." he eyeballed the fish, "about fourteen, maybe fifteen inches. Let's measure." It was far from being one of the ten pound lunkers frequently adorning the covers of fishing magazines, but it was definitely the biggest fish Jonas had ever landed. Rev. Harkness laid the fish on the ground at Jonas' feet and retrieved a measuring tape from his pocket. "Looks like... sixteen and a half! That's awesome, son. Good job!"

Jonas couldn't help but to grin like the Cheshire Cat. "Man, I can't wait to show momma."

"Here. Let's get a picture." said Rev. Harkness. "That's a whopper. Hold it high. There you go. Now smile." The flash discharged, and the moment was forever captured and converted to ones and zeros and stored on the memory card of the digital camera Rev. Harkness received as a birthday gift from the congregation. "Now go ahead, and turn him loose."

"We ain't gonna eat him?" Jonas asked.

"No, let him get bigger. We can come back next year, and he'll be huge. Besides, you know that feeling of pride you have from catching him? Don't you want other people to feel that? If you don't put him back, nobody else will have a chance to enjoy that same feeling."

After thinking, Jonas carried the fish to the edge of the water and bent over. He placed the fish into the water, holding it by its tail, and gently moved the fish backward and forward. The water moved through its gills to refresh it after the tiring fight and the time it spent out of the water. Within a second or two, the fish became excited and tried swimming away. Jonas released the tail, and the fish darted away into the bluish green waters of Teeter's Lake.

They continued fishing until the sun was high. Jonas caught two small bass, a handful of medium to large bluegills, and a rather large catfish, while Rev. Harkness caught three small bass. Rev. Harkness looked at his watch then reeled in his line.

"I guess Paul had your lunch, huh?" he said as he placed his pole on the ground and reached for the hand sanitizer in his tackle box.

"Yeah. I am kinda hungry. Should I call my momma?"

"Well, do you like bologna and cheese? I got three in the cooler here. I'll give you one. I've got some chips and a couple Cokes in there too." The reverend said rubbing his hands together.

"Sure, thanks," said Jonas, stowing his gear beside his chair.

"No problemo, kiddo," the reverend said, trying his best to be cool. "Y'know...it doesn't really get much better than this. A bright blue sky, a calm breeze, and cold Coke." He reached into the cooler and pulled out two plastic bottles of Coke.

"Paul don't know what he's missing," proclaimed Jonas, satisfied with his catch thus far. "He coulda been catching 'em all day. He's probably drunk on the couch right now."

"Well, I don't doubt it. But hey, how about that first one you caught? What a lunker, eh?"

"Yeah," Jonas replied between teeth covered in bologna and American cheese. "At first, I was afraid it would break the line and swim off, but I wrestled him in."

"You sure did. You think the afternoon will yield any better results?"

"Why not?" Jonas shrugged.

The two sat in their folding lawn chairs and silently

chewed on the sandwiches as they stared across the water. Rev. Harkness thought about what an ass Paul had made of himself and how badly he felt for Jonas. Meanwhile, Jonas thought about the fish he had caught and imagined it battered and fried, with fries, and a tall glass of Coke . The bologna and potato chips were sufficient, and they took away the rumble in his stomach.

Rev. Harkness interrupted, "Your momma says you made a new friend, huh?"

Jonas smacked his lips and took a swig from the Coke. "Yeah. He used to be a pastor, too. Last name is Chambers."

"I've heard of him. Never met him though. Your momma doesn't seem to like him."

"She don't like him. What did you hear?"

"I heard he got involved in some kinda money scam, and when people lost all their money, he quit. I heard his wife...well, you should probably ask Dolores about it all. It ain't my place to tell, seein' as how I don't know him properly."

"She said he's a liar and a thief, but I don't believe her. He seems like a nice, old man to me. He's never lied to me, and he's never stolen nothing from me. I don't know why Momma don't like him. He's nice. He even bought me an ice cream one day."

"Is that so?"

"Yep, because he almost left his hat on a bench, and I took it to him."

"Well, seems nice to me, I guess. I don't know, Jonas. Like I said, I've never met him, but your momma has. So I'd probably listen to her."

The two finished their sandwiches and Cokes, and in a few minutes they were fishing again. The afternoon was not as productive. They had a few bites between the two of them, but nobody caught anything. Even the boaters, who covered far more water than the shore fisherman, were disappointed by the fishing in the afternoon. By the early evening, everyone's resolve had broken and the boats started to return to the ramp. Those who kept the fish they caught proudly showed off their stringers of bass and blue gill. Dave Hawkins, a deacon in the church, had caught a twenty pound catfish. Rev. Harkness showed everyone the picture of Jonas' bass from early in the morning.

The reverend and Jonas loaded their gear in the back of the reverend's SUV and drove away to take Jonas home.

"You think Paul's gonna be home?" Rev. Harkness asked.

"I hope not. I hope he never comes back," Jonas replied. "He's so mean. I don't know why momma married him in the first place. He don't do nothin' but get drunk."

"Well, sometimes people are blinded by love, Jonas. They don't really see people for who they are because either they're lonely, or they want that person to fill some kinda void they have in their lives. Any number of reasons, actually. People do all kinds of crazy things for love. Between you and me, I don't care too much for him either. But Jesus does. Jesus loves him even though he treats people poorly." The reverend had a knack for turning every conversation into a sermon.

"I guess you're right. But it still don't change the fact that he's mean. I wish Jesus would make him act nicer. That would be a miracle."

"Ha! Well, I guess so, Jonas. Maybe tonight, when you say your prayers, you should ask God to open Paul's eyes so he can see how mean he's been. You never know, maybe you'll get that miracle. Don't know until you ask."

Once home, Jonas ran to the door to tell Dolores about the bass he caught. Dolores met the reverend at the door.

"Well, hey there!" she said, slightly confused as to where Paul was. "How was the day? Did you catch a big one?"

"You shoulda seen it, momma. It was huge! I fought with him and fought, but finally I reeled him in. Pastor's got pictures."

"Yep, look." He showed Dolores the pictures from the digital camera. "And there's some blue gills. Here's a monster ol' Hawkins caught. I tell you, every year he catches the big one. I think I might have to ask the board for a raise so I can get me a boat. Maybe I'll catch 'em the way he does." Rev. Harkness joked.

"Well, that's great! I'm glad you had fun. Listen, why don't you get washed up for supper, Jonas? I gotta talk to the pastor for a bit."

She walked Rev. Harkness out to his vehicle.

"Paul didn't stay?" she asked.

"No. I tell you what, that guy has got a temper. He was fishin' for maybe twenty minutes before he stormed off in a hissy about somethin'. The whole time he was really mean to Jonas. Is he like that when you're around?"

"No... I mean yes, but it's not like that. He's just a little grouchy. He works a lot, you know."

"Well, it's not my place to say anything, but that boy of yours is a great kid. Really is. It's a shame for Paul to be treatin' him like that. I didn't have a lick of a problem with Jonas all day. He's a good kid, Dolores, but he's coming up on puberty soon, and if whatever is going on between him and Paul ain't settled soon, I think he might end up getting himself into trouble. Y'know, lashing out, begging for attention and all. I've seen it a lot. You remember the Perkins boy? What was his name?"

"Jarvis."

"Yeah, Jarvis Perkins. He was the sweetest boy on the earth, just kind-hearted and gentle. Then puberty hit right around the time the Jenkins' got divorced, and he just went wild. Drinkin', smokin', runnin' with the wrong crowd. It's just that Jonas is a good boy, and I'd hate to have him go through what Jarvis did."

"Oh, I know. I know. Jonas is a good kid. And Paul does drink a lot. I've tried to get him to slow it down. He's just...well, he's just Paul. I don't know why I'm always makin' excuses for him. But he's never hit Jonas, or me for that matter. He's a hard worker, and when things are good, pastor, things are really good. He just gets a little alcohol in him, and he thinks the world should work the way he wants it to."

"Right. Right. Well listen, Dolores, if you ever need anything don't hesitate to call. You've got my home number and the church number. Just gimme a call if you need anything. I worry a lot about you and that boy."

"Thanks, pastor. Thanks again for keepin' an eye on Jonas. He really wanted to go so bad, and with Paul ducking out like that, I'm just glad he managed to turn it into a good time."

"No problem, Dolores. Anytime. Tell Jonas I said good night. I gotta get home and walk the dogs. You know Sue ain't gonna do it."

"At the next ladies meeting, I'm gonna tell her you said that," Dolores said jokingly.

"Alright, but I better start seeing Paul in the pew next to you two," he replied.

Dolores walked back inside the house and let the screen door shut behind her. She walked to the kitchen and checked on the fish sticks and french fries in the oven, and she set the table for two. She then sat down and sighed. She was disappointed in Paul, and she wondered where he could be. She had a few ideas and most of them involved the three bars in Allardale.

Chapter 8

The next day, Jonas and Dolores were on their way to church. The sun was bright and the sky was cloudless. It was a perfect summer day as she pulled her rusty blue sedan into the cemetery drive. She noticed Reverend Chambers walking towards Esther's grave as she pulled up under the maple tree.

"You just sit here," Dolores said to Jonas as she rolled down the windows and turned off the car. She tossed her keys into her purse and left it sitting between the seats. She marched directly toward Rev. Chambers, who by then had reached the grave of his late wife.

"Reverend? I don't know if you remember me. I'm Dolores Pike."

He turned to her, surprised. "Well, hello there. It's been a while, hasn't it?"

"Yeah, it has. Listen, I don't want to be late for service, so I'll make this quick. You need to stay away from Jonas, you hear me? After everything you've done to my family, I don't need you hanging around and ruining his life, too."

"I understand, Dolores. I didn't mean any harm. He was at the ice cream stand, and I was just making conversation."

"Well, don't. Don't. Just stay away," she said and walked back toward the car.

"Ain't you gonna talk to grandma?" Jonas asked as she

got into the car.

"No, we're running late, honey. Listen, I told you to stay away from that man. I don't want to hear you've been hanging around him. Got it?"

"Yeah," he replied. "Is it about all that money?"

She sighed heavily and started the car. "How do you know about the money?"

"He talked to me about it the other day."

"Yes, it's about that money. Jonas, he ripped us off. That's why you need to stay away from him. He's not a good man, Jonas. He stole all the money your grandparents had saved for their whole lives. He conned my momma into giving him their life savings, Jonas. Everything! Everything they had that they worked so hard for was gone, and he's the reason why your grandpa left."

"He is?"

"Honey, I was pregnant with you, and your grandpa was flat broke. He said he couldn't afford to take care of us all, and with all that money gone, he went off to Florida to go looking for a better job. I don't know what happened down there, but we never heard from him again. And it's all his fault," she said pointing toward Rev. Chambers. She slammed her hand on the steering wheel to fight back the tears.

"Momma, I don't think it's all his fault. He lost money, too."

"But he didn't have to go talking everybody in the

church into losing their money, too. Honey, just listen to me and stay away from him. He's no good."

Jonas looked at Rev. Chambers through the window as Dolores pulled away from the maple tree. He had every intention of disobeying Dolores. He saw the old minister for who he really was: a spiritually broken man who simply fell victim to a con artist. There was something about the old man that Jonas saw but couldn't define. Jonas knew what it was like to be an outcast, and in that respect he saw Rev. Chambers as a brother-in-arms, someone who needed his help.

Chapter 9

Dolores tugged on the collar of her coat and fluffed her scarf to guard her neck against the cold December wind, which was making her walk to school dreary and miserable. But then again, ever since that night at the cabin two months ago, pretty much everything seemed dreary and miserable to her. She never reported the rape. She didn't tell her parents; they were mad enough that she came home smelling like booze and vomit, and she was afraid they'd never believe her, or even worse, blame her for what had happened. And she certainly didn't tell the police. Like the boys said, who would the cops believe? She didn't even tell her best friend Sandy Malone, whose house she was approaching on her way to school.

Sandy was a good friend to Dolores. They had met in the third grade when Sandy and her parents moved into the huge Victorian home on Hampton Street next door to Rev. Chambers'. Much like the other old houses in Allardale, it was in desperate need of repairs after having been converted from a single family home into two apartments many years before. The years of neglectful tenants, and even more neglectful landlords, had taken its toll on the once stately home. But Mr. Malone was an excellent carpenter, and he and Mrs. Malone had big plans for the renovation. It took them nearly ten years, but they finally had returned the house to its prior glory, with wrought iron gates and all.

Dolores had reached the stairs of the porch when Sandy came bounding out of the front door, her blonde hair bouncing in a pony tail behind her.

"Hey Dory!" she said cheerfully. "I can't believe it's almost Christmas already. I love, love, love the winter. Doesn't get much better than this."

"It's freezing out. Are you nuts?"

"Nah, this is the best time of year. Just wait until we get a decent amount of snow. It looks prettier all covered in white."

"I guess." Dolores looked around. The town seemed dead to her. The trees had long ago shed their leaves, and all of the grass was brown. She found it depressing, much like everything else since that night in the cabin.

"You okay? You seem, like, out of it or something." Sandy had noticed the sudden change in her friend two months ago but hadn't said anything, assuming she would tell her when she was ready.

"Yeah, I'm just kinda sick."

"Oh, well there is a cold going around. Everybody's got the sniffles in my Girl Scout troop. Even Haley, and she never gets sick."

"No, it's not a cold. I'm just sick to my stomach. I dunno what it is. Maybe I ate something. I dunno, it doesn't matter."

Sandy decided to finally get nosy. "Look, Dory, I don't

know what's bothering you, but you've been a real Debby Downer for awhile now. I'm your best friend, if something's bothering you, I should know about it. I can't help you if you won't let me."

Dolores looked at her and back down at the ground. She wanted to tell her about Lane, Skeeter and the boys, but she couldn't. She didn't even know how to begin.

"I feel your pain." Sandy said in her best impression of Bill Clinton. Dolores usually laughed heartily when Sandy did impressions, but this time she could only manage a chuckle. Her stomach was churning, which reminded her of the last time she threw up.

"Okay, you don't wanna tell me. That's your business. But I'm here if you need me. You know that."

"Thanks, Sandy." Dolores said and left it at that. She instantly regretted not coming clean to her about being raped. She didn't know how her friend would react, and she didn't want to risk losing a good friend.

The two girls reached the high school and parted ways once inside to go toward their respective lockers. Dolores never arrived at hers; her stomach wouldn't allow it. She darted toward the girls' room, dropped her books onto the floor, and heaved into the toilet. The English teacher, Mrs. Carson, was in the restroom and heard Dolores in the stall. She knocked on the stall door.

"Are you okay in there?"

Dolores spit to get rid of the remnants of breakfast from

her mouth and quickly unrolled some toilet paper to clean up. "Yeah, I'll be fine," she gasped as she gathered her books and opened the stall door.

"Why don't you go on down to the office and wait for the nurse. She'll be here in about a half hour."

"No, really, I'll be okay. I've got a midterm in Geography that I can't afford to miss. I'm fine." But she wasn't. Another wave of nausea hit her, and she shoved her books at Mrs. Carson and ran back into the stall for another round of heaving, gasping, and spitting.

When the noise from the flushing toilet quieted down, she said, "Dolores, you really should go to the office. You can't take a test in this condition, and if you're sick, you don't want to pass it on to anyone else."

Dolores mulled over the idea for a minute while she cleaned up and decided that it was probably for the best to go see the nurse.

Dolores was uncomfortable in the office. Besides having an upset stomach, she could count on one hand the number of times she had been in the office, so the unfamiliarity of the room bothered her. Her gaze shifted from the motivational posters on the wall to the scuffs on her sneakers to the secretary who was stamping some type of forms while talking on the phone. After what seemed like an eternity, the school nurse, Mrs. Bellamy, came through the door. Without missing a beat in her conversation, the secretary motioned toward Dolores.

"C'mon back, hon. We'll take a look-see," she said, and Dolores followed her.

The nurse's office was even more unfamiliar to Dolores than the school office. She rarely, if ever, got sick. She hadn't even missed a single day of school since the fifth grade when she had to take off two days for a tonsillectomy. The walls were covered in medical posters showing the muscle structure of the human body and various pictures of cross sections of organs, as well as posters advising students to not use drugs or smoke. Another had a black and white image of police at the scene of an auto accident. Beneath the picture in big red letters it simply read, "Don't Drink and Drive."

Mrs. Bellamy placed her coat on the coat rack and locked her purse in a cabinet under the drawer labeled "Bandages". "Go ahead and have a seat. What brings you in?" she asked as she washed her hands.

"I'm sick. I threw up twice this morning before the bell even rang."

"Well, that's no good. Let me check your temperature," she said as she placed the back of her hand against Dolores' forehead. "No fever. What did you have to eat for breakfast?"

"Just a bowl of cereal. But the milk was good, I checked the date."

"Hmm. What about last night? What did you have for

dinner? Any fish or shrimp or anything?" she asked as she felt the sides on Dolores neck.

"No, just chicken, mashed potatoes, green beans."

"Okay, well, I'm running out of ideas here. Might just be a bug that's been going around. There is one other... has your period been regular?"

Dolores blushed. "No, it didn't come in November. Usually it's toward the end of the month, but I figured it was just late."

"Well, honey, I suggest that if you're sexually active you go to your doctor and get checked. You might be pregnant," she said with a frown.

Panic shot through Dolores' body. She had been trying so hard for the last two months to forget about the rape that she hadn't even considered the possibility of a pregnancy resulting from it. The next thought she had was fear. Her mother would definitely freak out if she asked to go to the doctor for a pregnancy test, and the questions which would result would be too much to answer.

"Okay, I will," she said dismissively, imagining that the nurse assumed she was promiscuous.

"But for today, you should probably just head home, drink plenty of liquids, and get some rest. You can use the phone up front to call your folks to pick you up."

"They're at work. Can I just walk home?"

"If you're gonna do that, you need to stay in the office

for awhile so we can make sure you don't get any worse. Don't want you passing out or anything on the way home."

Dolores sat in the hard plastic chairs in the waiting area of the office. Her stomach was empty, but she periodically felt the urge to heave and held her breath to try to make it abate. She waited until two minutes before the bell, then she put her hand to her mouth as if she was going to vomit and ran toward the bathroom. When she got toward the end of the hallway, out of sight of the school secretary, she walked past the bathroom. Instead, she turned left down the science hallway toward the classroom from which Sandy was about to be released. She poked her head toward the small window in the door and looked around the class for her. Sandy saw Dolores, looked at the clock on the wall, and held up one finger before returning her attention to the teacher.

Soon the bell rang, and students began filing out of the door to the class. Dolores grabbed Sandy by the arm and pulled her aside.

"I need to borrow some money, no questions asked."

"Now, you know I'm gonna ask questions," Sandy smiled and rolled her eyes.

"No, I mean it. I'll pay you back, I swear. I just really, REALLY need to borrow ten bucks. Pleeeeease?"

Sandy rummaged through her purse and pulled out a twenty dollar bill. She extended it to Dolores, and then pulled it back. "You don't have to pay me back if you tell me what the heck is going on."

"I will, I promise. Just not now."

"You're not in trouble?"

Dolores looked around and stepped closer to Sandy.

"Sandy, if I tell you something, can you PROMISE not to say anything to anyone?"

"Dory, c'mon! I'm gonna be late to class."

"Okay, if you swear not to tell anyone... I think I might be pregnant, and I need to buy one of those pregnancy test thingies that you pee on."

Sandy's jaw dropped. "Ooooooh! I knew it, I knew it! Something was different about you. Here. I gotta get to class," she said as she shoved the twenty into Dolores' hands, "but you owe me an explanation later." She added as she walked away, "WITH DETAILS!"

Dolores tucked the money into her pocket and walked back to the office to get her books. The secretary glanced at her over her glasses.

Dolores avoided eye contact, gathered her books, signed herself out on the clipboard, and headed toward the drug store.

At the store, she hung out by the magazines for nearly two hours, thumbing slowly through each one, waiting for the cashier to go on break. The cashier, Ethel Myers, knew her mother, and even worse, she was a horribly nosy old woman. If someone needed to get the word out about something to the entire population of Allardale as soon as humanly possible, that person would go see Ethel. Between her quilting club, bridge club, women's club at the church, and the other blue hairs who met her weekly at the salon, Dolores figured her mother would be calling the house before she even got home with the test kit.

When she saw the old woman leave the register and walk to the back room, she felt the time was right, and Dolores darted toward the aisle where the pregnancy tests were. She stood back to weigh her options, quickly decided on the brand with the plus or minus sign, and walked toward the register, her eyes ever vigilant for any sign of Ethel.

She paid for the test, stuffed it into her purse, grabbed the change, and ran home. Once home, she sprinted to the bathroom and tore into the box. She read the instructions twice, went to the kitchen and drank two glasses of water, then back to the bathroom to read the instructions yet again and wait for the urge to go. When she could no longer hold it in, she took the test according to the instructions and carefully placed the test on the box on the bathroom counter, and then she waited. After what seemed like an eternity, a faint blue plus sign slowly began to appear. Dolores slumped onto the edge of the tub and sobbed into her hands, a million thoughts racing through her mind.

When she was done, Dolores gathered the test, the empty box and the instructions, crushed them into a ball, wrapped it in foil to hide the evidence from her parents, and tucked it into the bottom of the trash can in the garage. She wasn't sure what she would do next, who she would tell, or how she would tell them, but she knew eventually she would have to tell her parents, and that scared her more than anything.

Chapter 10

Sandy was waiting on the porch for Dolores the next
morning.

"Well?" she asked nervously.

Dolores thought for a moment about how to word it
while she sat down on the porch next to Sandy. The best she
came up with was a reluctant, "Yes."

"Oh my God, Dory! Did you tell your folks? Who was
it? Is he cute? What was it like? Is it like in the movies, all
romantic and stuff? C'mon, give me details, girlfriend."

"No, it was nothing like that." She began the story she
concocted to hide her shame. "It was this guy from that
youth group in Marietta I told you about. Our church and his
church met up for a gathering, and we snuck off and did it."

Sandy gasped, "In the church?!"

Dolores didn't think of that. "No. In his car."

"He has a car? What's his name? So is he cute? When
do I get to meet him?"

"Sandy, stop. You don't get to meet him. It was a one-
time thing, and I'm probably never going to see him again.
It's not a big deal. I'm just gonna have to deal with it, that's
all. I'm pregnant, and I'm just gonna have to deal with it."

Sandy leaned toward her and hugged her. "Well, if you
need anything, just call. You know I'm here for you."

"Thanks. Now I just have to figure out how to tell my
parents. They're already fighting about all that money they

lost. This is just great."

"You want me to come with? I can help you tell 'em if that's what you're thinking."

"No, I don't know. God, I don't know. What am I gonna do? I mean, I've never even changed a diaper!"

"You're a woman, Dory. It'll come naturally. We're more caring and stuff. But, wow! Oh my God! I can't believe it. That's kinda cool, in a weird way."

"Not cool, Sandy. Not cool at all. I'm gonna get all fat, and the stretch marks..." Dolores started crying again. "And my parents are gonna KILL me! Seriously, I can't even begin to think of how they're gonna punish me for this. Remember when I broke that window? They grounded me for weeks! They're gonna flip! I just know it."

"I'm sure it's pretty scary. I didn't mean cool, but seriously though, you have another human being growing inside of you. THAT is pretty damn cool."

"Yeah," she sniffed and managed a smile as she put her hand on her belly.

"So have you thought of any names?"

"You're, like, a million miles ahead of me here, Sandy. Let me get used to the idea of being pregnant first. Then let me figure out how to tell my folks. Then maybe we can figure out names. Besides, I don't even know if it's gonna be a boy or a girl yet."

"Well, anyway, I hope it's a girl."

"I just hope it's healthy." Then she gasped. "Oh God, Sandy! What if it's born with fins instead of hands? I saw a kid on TV like that."

"I'm sure it'll be healthy," said Sandy reassuringly. "It's got a good momma."

Chapter 11

It had rained overnight, which left the air thick and sticky. Jonas was riding his bike down Cambden Street and was thinking about Rev. Chambers. He wondered why everyone seemed to either hate or ignore the old man even though to Jonas, he had been nothing but kind and generous. He decided to find the old man to ask him about it. He figured he had to go straight to the source to get any real answers.

He took off toward the school, leaning his bike alternately left and right with each   heavy downward stroke of the pedals. Like every boy with a little bit of freedom and a set of wheels, he thought he was cool. He remembered the detective on TV with the fast muscle car and the dark sunglasses. He leaned into each corner and came out of the turns pedaling hard and fast. He was on a case, chasing clues, searching for the truth.

Jonas rounded the last corner by the ice cream stand where he first spoke with Rev. Chambers. He pulled hard on the brakes, lowered his body, leaned left and let the back tire come out from under him in a wide, screeching arc. Dolores would often yell at him for skidding his tires that way. "Jonas, do you have money to buy new tires?" she would ask him. But this time she wasn't around, and neither was Rev. Chambers. He continued down the street and turned right, cutting through the park. There was no sign of the reverend there, either. Feeling his search was becoming fruitless, Jonas decided to do a little detective work the old-fashioned way: research. He took off toward the convenience store where a payphone (the only one that hadn't been gotten rid of) was affixed to a pole between the parking lot and the sidewalk. It was old, and the paint had long been chipped from the shroud which barely protected it from the elements. All over the shroud, in predominately black permanent marker, teenagers had tagged their names and aliases. Some phone numbers were scribbled on it, some with just a first name, and others had "For a good time call..." written above it. Someone with exquisite penmanship had written a poem about loneliness and alienation with a red paint marker on the ledge which sat above the phone book which was secured to a thick metal cable. Jonas hated poems, but he hated even more the fact that someone had ripped out the phone book entirely. He kicked the pole upon which the phone was mounted, turned his bike around, and headed home to look up the old man's address.

He rode back through the park, down the street toward the ice cream stand, around the corner by the video store, cut through the parking lot of the gas station, and turned left on Cambden Street toward home. He let his bike fall to the ground while he ran inside to find the phone book. Dolores had a habit of not returning the phone book to the drawer next to the phone in the kitchen, so Jonas had to search for it.

It wasn't on top of the fridge or the microwave. There was nothing on the end tables in the living room, so he sifted through old issues of women's magazines under the coffee table. The covers were all torn off because it was Dolores' job to do so to all of the expired magazines at the grocery store and dispose of them in the trash. Occasionally she would find an article or a recipe she wanted to keep, so she would tuck the magazine into her purse and bring it home. Under the coffee table was the repository for almost two years' worth of coverless magazines.

Jonas finally found the phone book in the bathroom, which he thought was odd since they didn't have a cordless phone. "1020 Carlisle," he repeated to himself over and over so he wouldn't forget, and he went back outside to get his bike.

Once Jonas found Rev. Chambers' house, he stopped his bike on the sidewalk near the walkway to the door. He got off the bike and walked it toward the wide, neglected porch. The reverend happened to catch a glimpse of Jonas coming toward the porch and opened the front door.

"Jonas," he said cheerfully, "what brings you here?"

"I've got questions. Hard questions."

The reverend chuckled at such a forward response from such a young boy. "Well, if it's alright with your mom, you can have a seat here on the porch. I'll go get something to drink. You look thirsty."

Jonas climbed the stairs to the porch and sat on the wicker love seat. In a moment, the reverend came back with a glass of sweet tea. He handed Jonas the glass and sat down across from him on a wicker chair.

"Does your mom know you're here?"

"No, she told me to stay away from you. She said you're no good, but I don't believe her. She'd be mad if she knew I was here."

"So what is important enough to disobey your mother and ride your bike all the way over here to talk to me? Bullies? Girls?"

"No," Jonas blushed, "it's about you. How come Momma hates you?"

Rev. Chambers was taken aback. He let out a big sigh and replied, "Well, geez, I told you about the con artist, right? Well, a lot of folks lost a lot of money, and they blame me for it. Rightly so, I guess."

"But it wasn't your fault. You were trying to do something good for everyone."

"Yeah, that's true, but in the process I hurt a lot of people. Things don't always turn out according to your intentions, Jonas."

"But it was their decision to give that guy all that money. You didn't make em do it, did you?"

"No, no, I didn't force anybody to do anything. But I did persuade people- people who I was supposed to be taking care of and looking out for. I was their pastor, you see. I was their shepherd, and they were my flock. A shepherd is supposed to look after the flock, to keep them from danger- physical and spiritual danger. I suppose my greatest fault is in betraying their trust. Causing them to lose their faith."

"How can they lose their faith? It's something you believe in, not something like your car keys."

"Yeah, but by betraying them about something so important as their finances, they lost their trust in me, and subsequently, their trust in God. Myself included."

"But you're a pastor."

"Used to be."

"Okay, used to be a pastor. Still, it's your job to have faith, right?"

"Yeah, but when I needed my faith the most, it seemed like it wasn't there for me. Like someone just came and took it from me. I honestly believed that God would bless us for our faithfulness and reward our good works, but it turned out to be a scam. That got me thinking, what else have I always held onto as a sure thing that might not be so? And then the Mrs went and did what she did, and that was the proverbial straw that broke the camel's back, see? I had enough. I turned to God in my hour of need, and it seemed like he ignored me. So I retired from the ministry, and I've spent the rest of my time here trying to figure it all out."

"Hmm," said Jonas contemplatively, "well you're wrong, Reverend Chambers."

The reverend choked on his tea. "Well, then..."

"You're wrong. God didn't fail you. You had faith, and He's gonna help you. You can't just give up like that."

"That's easy for you to say."

"If you give up, you've definitely lost your faith, and that means you have no hope. If you have no hope, you might as well go jump in the lake. You have to believe, Reverend. You have to."

"And how do you suppose I go about doing that?"

Jonas thought for a bit. "I don't know exactly. But I'll think of something. I'll go home and think about it, and I'll meet you at the park tomorrow around noon."

Reverend Chambers humored him. "Alright, then. Tomorrow at noon."

Chapter 12

It was late May, and the school was electrified with the promise of summer. The teachers had all been frustrated at the students' lack of concentration over the past few weeks, an academically debilitating illness the faculty had termed "summer-itis". But while the students neglected their studies to plan their summer escapades, Dolores was hard at work at the Food Lion grocery store. She had dropped out of school in order to work to help out with the bills at home. Her father had left her and her mother to fend for themselves when the news of her pregnancy, coupled with the loss of their savings in the pyramid scheme at the church, had become too much for him to bear.

She was standing near the front entrance of the store, organizing the shopping carts and baskets and gathering the loose sales fliers which the shoppers had left scattered among the carts. She placed a basket on the top of the stack and happened to glance at the newspaper rack beside it. The local newspaper had a full page write up on Lane Sherman and his scholarship to Brighton. Immediately, her stomach turned, and she waddled to the restrooms as quickly as her seven-months-pregnant body would allow.

"You oughta be done with that puking phase by now, Dory," said Mary Roundtree, her coworker who was wasting time by hiding in the restroom. The store's manager called it, "riding the clock by riding the can".

"No, it's not morning sickness. I got over that awhile ago. It's just something didn't smell right over by the produce."

"I was gonna say, honey, cause I got over my morning sickness after, like, the end of the third month. After that it was smooth sailing... well, other than the backaches, the sore feet, the swelling legs, and that toxo-somethin er other."

She meant well, but Mary wasn't really helping matters much.

"I'll be fine," Dolores sniffed, "but I'm gonna need a minute, if you could."

After finally sensing that she was intruding, Mary turned around and left Dolores to herself. Dolores, meanwhile, wondered if the emotions of that night at the cabin would ever fade. She wasn't naive enough to think they would go away completely, or that one day she would wake up having forgotten that the incident ever happened. No, she was constantly reminded of that night by the ever-growing, always kicking lump in her belly, and every now and again by a random stranger's cologne. But now, having read the name of the chief instigator of the vicious attack on her, and seeing how he was being hailed as a big time football hero, she begged God to make her forget. And while they didn't go away completely, within a few moments the memories sank just slightly under the surface, just enough for Dolores to regain her composure and concentrate on her work. She had more baskets to organize and an entire rack of magazines to sort, so she washed her face and waddled back toward the front of the store.

Later, while pricing a cereal box display, she overheard two old men talking about the article.

"I tell you, he's got great hands," said the taller one.

"Yeah, but he's a troublemaker. He'd do better to go to a bigger school. More of a chance of them keeping him straight," said the other.

"But a small school is where he'd be the big fish."

"Big fish, big shmish. If he plays for them, he'll be the spoiled kid, and he'll end up getting into trouble. Remember that goat of mine that he and the cop's kid stole from me? It'll be worse with all that fame going to his head. A bigger school will put him in his place, give him some perspective. Mature him a little."

"That cop's kid, whats-his-name?"

"Skeeter's what they call him. Dunno his real name."

"Yeah, Skeeter. He's a hell of a big boy on that line. Where's he going?"

"Oh, I dunno. Last I heard, he's planning on moving to North Carolina to work for his uncle. You remember Dave Simmons? Chief Simmons' brother. Played ball back in the 80's?"

"No, I can't place him."

"Well, that's that kids' uncle. He moved to North

Carolina and started a towing company."

"And he's not gonna be playing for a college? So he can tow cars around? What a waste. A big boy like that oughta be playing ball somewhere."

Dolores quickly finished pricing the display items and returned to her register. She was somewhat relieved to think that both Lane and Skeeter would soon be far away.

Soon, however, wasn't soon enough. A week later, Dolores was running the cash register when Lane and Skeeter appeared at the back of the line. She hadn't seen either of them since she dropped out of school. They didn't immediately recognize her, but she instantly recognized them. When she did, she found herself suddenly immobile. Her entire body was frozen as if she was a mannequin, and she lost her grip on the jar of pickles she had just scanned. She didn't hear it hit the floor and shatter because her ears were filled with the sound of her own heart beating violently. Her vision closed in around her, and a metal taste came to her tongue. Her eyes rolled back, her knees buckled and she fell to the floor like a sack of dirty laundry. The store manager heard a commotion from the customers and saw Dolores on the floor, and he ran to her register to help.

"Give her some room! Call an ambulance!" he shouted as he squatted over her with outspread arms, even though the only person crowding her was himself. He quickly knelt beside her shoulders and bent over close to her face to check for breath. He heard her breathing and sat up to check her pulse. Her heart was still beating, and a quick examination didn't reveal any cuts from the broken jar. "Did she hit her head as she fell?" he turned to ask the old woman who was leaning over the conveyor. The look on her face seemed to suggest she was more concerned about her broken jar of pickles than the welfare of Dolores. She could only recall that it "happened so fast" that she couldn't say for sure.

The ambulance arrived in a few minutes, and Dolores was still unconscious. The EMTs quickly loaded her onto a gurney and carried her to the hospital. She awoke to the harsh glare of fluorescent lights and the all-encompassing scent of disinfectant.

"You've been mumbling for a good twenty minutes now. I figured you'd be awake soon," said the blurry figure whom Delores correctly assumed was a nurse. She was poking at a blurry box with blurry lights and writing on her blurry clipboard.

"Wha... what happened?" asked Dolores.

"You fainted at the grocery store, hon. You were out cold. And with you being pregnant and all, they figured they'd bring you here. You're gonna be OK, and the baby's just fine. I'll let the doctor know you're up, and he'll be right in to answer any questions. Oh, and your boss called your mother, so she's on her way."

The nurse walked out of the room before Dolores' vision had completely returned.

"Fainted," grumbled Dolores incredulously as she placed her hand on her head. She squinted at the ceiling and blinked a few times to clear her vision. She looked around the small room at all of the equipment and government mandated signs. Her clothes were in a plastic grocery bag on a chair next to the hand sink. She slowly started recalling what had happened prior to her unconsciousness, and she became embarrassed. She wasn't embarrassed because she fainted at the sight of her attackers, but more because she felt she made a fool of herself in front of her coworkers and all of the customers. Her attackers know why her body simply could not tolerate their very existence in that spot at that moment, but as for the others, they were clueless. They would be wondering and guessing what caused it and whether she's she was OK. She would have to make up an excuse, and even worse, have to retell that lie for as many times as she was asked, "What happened?" But to invent a lie and have to re-tell it a million times would still be easier than to admit the truth. And so Dolores reclined back into the hospital bed, waited for the doctor, and hoped he'd provide her with an excuse before her mother arrived.

Chapter 13

Jonas was on his way to meet Reverend Chambers at the park. The tires of his bicycle were making a soft buzz against the blacktop, a buzz which pulsated in tone, in perfect cadence with every downward stroke of the pedals. The midday air was hot and thick with humidity. A sweat,which at first was barely a moistening of Jonas' forehead, had progressed beyond an occasional drop spilling over his brow, and had now become a glistening mask which covered his face and ran down his neck. He was out of breath, and the sidewalk ran slightly uphill going toward the park bench where Rev. Chambers sat. While holding the handlebars, Jonas threw his right leg back and over to the left side of the wheel and hopped off the pedal with the left, causing him to have to jog for a few steps until the bike slowed down to his walking speed. The reverend waited patiently for Jonas to come to him, not wanting to strain himself in the midday sun on what was turning out to be the hottest day of the year. That kind of heat could kill younger and stronger men.

"Hey, Reverend," panted Jonas.

"Awful hot to be riding that hard. Let's walk on down back to the corner and get some ice cream. My treat."

Jonas wiped his forehead. "Yeah, please. Thanks."

"So did you think of any plans for our dilemma?"

"Nothing solid. I'm still thinking, though."

Reverend Chambers laughed.

"What?"

"Oh, nothing. Yesterday you sounded like you had a rock solid plan in the works. I'm sure we'll figure something out."

"Well, I was kinda thinking..."

"So you do have a plan?"

"I mean, it's not really a plan, plan. It's just some ideas running around in my head. Nothing solid, like I said."

"Well, it sounds like you want to spit it out, so let's order our ice cream, and sit down over there in the shade. You can figure out what you wanna say when the sun ain't baking your brain."

"Yeah," Jonas laughed as he wiped more sweat from his forehead and walked to the side of the ice cream shop to lean his bike against the picnic table under the umbrella.

"Two small vanillas, please," the reverend said through the window. He turned to say something to Jonas, but forgot what it was when he saw Jonas covered in sweat. He turned back around to the window and said, "Could you make those larges? Thanks."

"Really, sir, I'm fine with just a small," Jonas said politely.

"Ah, don't worry about it," the reverend said with a wave. "It's hot out, and I think we both could use a little something extra to cool us down."

"Good then. Cuz I do my best thinking after eating some ice cream. More ice cream, better ideas."

"That's the best thought you've had so far, Jonas."

They waited patiently despite the heat. They could feel the heat radiating from the blacktop in the street, the concrete sidewalk, and the sun above them. Every car that passed cast a swift, blinding glare toward where Jonas and Reverend Chambers were standing. After a few moments, two female hands poked through the window, each clutching a large vanilla ice cream cone as if the hands were bestowing enormous, frozen dairy scepters upon the anxious pair.

"When you say large, they sure give you a large," said Reverend Chambers, surprised at the size of the cones.

They took their cones and walked around to the side of the building. They sat at the table where Jonas had leaned his bike. They were mostly silent while they ate, only occasionally would one or the other let out a groan of enjoyment while they licked the drips, which due to the heat, was becoming a more pressing concern than actually eating the ice cream itself.

Jonas finished the last bite of his cone, wiped his mouth, wrinkled the napkin into a ball, and said, "So here's what I'm thinking," before swallowing.

"I figure at church, the pastor says that somewhere in the Bible it says that faith without works is dead. So I think if you want to have your faith back, you need to go around doing good deeds and whatnot."

"Sounds good. But what if I go do all these good deeds and still don't have any faith?" the reverend asked, still eating his cone.

"See that's the thing, Reverend. If you didn't have faith you wouldn't be doing the good deeds to begin with. I don't think you lost your faith so much as you just forgot how to trust it."

"So you think doing nice things for some people will help me?"

"It can't hurt. What's the worst that could happen?" asked Jonas.

"Let me tell you, it's pretty funny you thought of that. After our talk yesterday, I did a lot of thinking myself. Still don't have a plan, but I'm still thinking. But I thought about pretty much the same thing. I figured after the mess I made and the missus dying, I got pretty hung up on myself and stopped doing things for others. Pretty selfish, I guess."

"Eh, I dunno. I would have been pretty mad if all that stuff happened to me."

"I'm not talking about mad, Jonas. I'm talking about being completely disillusioned with church, God, and pretty much everything. Just being so overwhelmed that I couldn't even imagine doing anything for anyone because I was too busy being consumed with my misery. Maybe doing for others instead of focusing on me will do my old soul some good."

"Alright, well it sounds like we agree. Now we gotta pick someone out for you to do something nice for." Jonas sat and thought. "What about Old Lady Hopkins? She always needs help with the garden, and tells my mom all the time that I should go over and help her. I don't want to, though, because she smells funny."

"But I don't think it's as simple as that, Jonas. I mean, how can years of pain and suffering be overcome by just one little act of charity? Technically, charity doesn't even require faith, just a healthy sense of guilt."

"Well, you said you were feeling guilty, right? So go help someone you've done wrong. That's where you need to start."

Reverend Chambers mulled over the names of a few people who immediately popped into mind, then quickly rejected the entire notion. "How naive am I?" he thought. He had trouble believing that any advice from a kid would be helpful in the first place. But something about Jonas' sincerity made him want to believe.

Wanting to change the subject, Reverend Chambers asked, "Can I ask you something, Jonas?"

"Sure."

"I'm not making fun, or being mean or anything, I'm just kinda curious. And please, if you're not comfortable talking about it, then we don't have to. But...well, what happened to your jaw, son?"

"Born like this. Doctor said it's a deposit of calcium. I take medicine but it's probably never going to go away, he says."

"Does it hurt any?"

"Nah, just tingles every now and then. Sometimes if I sleep on it wrong, it'll hurt in the morning. But not really."

"Do the other kids at school tease you about it?"

"They used to, sometimes. But they all know me now, and they're used to it, I guess. It doesn't bother me now."

"See, that's what I mean, Jonas. I don't understand why God, if he's all-powerful, and loving, and kind, why would he force you to go through something like that? That's what I mean when I say I'm disillusioned. I don't get it. I mean, sure, if God wanted to toss some wrath on me for what I did, that's fine, because I deserved it. But what did you do to deserve a lifelong deformity?"

"Momma says it builds character. Makes me a better person."

"But even if that's true, why couldn't you have been given some adversity to overcome, which didn't involve something so glaringly and painfully obvious? I don't mean to hurt your feelings by talking about it. I just figured it made a good example for what I was talking about."

"You didn't hurt my feelings. Seriously, I only think about it when I'm at the doctor's. Half the time, I don't even remember what I'm taking medicine for unless I look in the mirror."

"Well, it sure has built your character. You're a much stronger young man than I would be, given the same situation. I guess – I mean, I don't really know because I haven't been through it. But you know what I'm saying, right?"

"Pastor says God doesn't give anybody a burden they can't handle. I guess he just made me extra good at handling this one."

Chapter 14

The night air was warm and damp. The window in
Jonas' bedroom was open, allowing the song of the crickets
to make its way in. The pale, blue moonlight shined through
the window onto the posters of sports cars which were tacked
to the wall opposite the window. The room was just big
enough to fit Jonas' single bed, a small shelf for his
keepsakes and books, and a dresser. The room was longer
than it was wide, and in the summer Jonas pushed his bed
from under the posters to against the window so he could
feel the breeze. That particular night, Jonas was fast asleep
under the window. He had kicked his sheet to the foot of the
bed and was lying flat on his back, in only his underwear, his
arms loosely folded above his head.

Behind the headboard, and on the other side of the wall,
crickets could be heard through the open window in the
bedroom which Dolores and Paul shared. The room was
small, and square, with a queen size, four-post bed taking up
most of the floor space. Her dresser and nightstand matched
the bed, and both were kept meticulously tidy. On the top of
her dresser were her purse and a 5x7 of Jonas's most recent
school picture. On her night stand sat an alarm clock. In the
top drawer were three coverless women's magazines, a bottle
of ibuprofen, and the container which held her birth control
pills. Paul's dresser, however, served as both the storage
space for his clothes and the depository for fishing

magazines, girly magazines, tool catalogs, spare change, a pocketknife, his keys, his wallet, two cell phone chargers to phones he no longer owned, a trophy from his bowling league, a Siltwell Feed ball cap, four crumpled and empty cigarette packs, a half empty glass of orange juice, two beef jerky wrappers, the cardboard tube from a roll of toilet paper, a broken pair of scissors, a ticket from a rock concert three years ago, a calendar from two years ago which features hot rods on scenic roads, a half dozen ink pens, stray paper clips and rubber bands, and as if it were a cargo strap, his leather belt was laid across the pile. It was a cheap dresser, made of fiberboard and veneer, with a cardboard back, and held together with glue and a handful of screws which were almost guaranteed to work themselves out of their holes, if not strip them out entirely.

Paul was sitting up in bed, reading a hunting magazine while Dolores was still getting undressed.

"Man, I want one of these four wheelers." Paul mumbled.

"Can you fix my air conditioning first, hon?" she replied.

"I said I will, just give me some time."

"Well, it's just that you said you'd do it last summer, and you kept putting it off. This summer is in full swing, and I'm sweating like a whore in church when I drive to work. You said it was an easy fix, so I don't understand why you haven't fixed it yet."

"Jesus Christ, woman," he groaned as he dropped the magazine into his lap. "If you keep nagging me about it, I'll NEVER do it, just to spite you."

"Oh, that's mature."

"I didn't know we were having a contest to see who was more mature. What are you? In seventh grade still? You gonna make your finger and thumb into a "L" and put it on your forehead? Keep it up, woman, see what happens."

"Like what, Paul? You gonna actually end up doing the things you say you're gonna do, when you say you're going to do them? That'll be the day."

She lifted the covers from her side of the bed and slid one leg under the sheet when Paul tossed the magazine on the floor, grabbed her around the waist, and pulled her on top of him. "How about I say I'm gonna make sweet, sweet love to you all night long? Then actually do it?"

She laughed and kissed him. "Do you promise to fix the air? And, like, soon?"

"Promise, cross my heart, scouts honor and all that stuff."

"We'll that sounds like a deal, then," she said as she reached across his side of the bed to turn off the lamp.

Dolores sat up and crossed her arms around her waist to remove her shirt, but she was interrupted by the phone ringing.

"Who the hell?" grunted Paul.

Dolores shushed him as she reached for her purse. Light from the phone's display shot out of her purse when she unzipped it. She flipped it open without looking and said hello.

The voice on the other end said, "Uh, is Jeff there?"

She took the phone away from her ear and stared at the number on the display. "Wrong number," she said, and she hung up.

"Who were they looking for?" asked Paul while he played with himself.

"I dunno. Somebody named Jeff," she said. Her stomach rumbled. "Honey, can I give you a rain check tonight? My stomach doesn't feel so hot. I think it was dinner."

"OK, now I definitely want to know who the fuck it was. Let me see your phone."

"It's a wrong number. Don't worry about it."

"Five seconds ago, you were all hot and bothered, and now you're sick to your stomach. I heard him say your name, Dory. Are you cheating on me? Who the hell –"

"Nobody, Paul. They had the wrong number. You didn't hear me say that?"

"Well, what the hell is some dude calling here at night for? Cock blocking me, what the hell? Why is he calling here at all?"

"I don't know, honey. Just please, I'm sick to my

stomach, I told him wrong number, so he won't be calling back. I'll talk to you about it tomorrow. I assure you, I'm not cheating on you. I promise."

"Better not be, goddamn it. I swear, if you ever did, I'd shoot the both of you. And I mean that. I'll shoot you, and him, and I'll burn the place to the fuckin' ground."

"Well, lucky for me then, because I'm not cheating on you. I swear, sometimes you get so..." she said and walked into the bathroom to splash some water on her face.

"So, what?"

"So jealous, I mean for crying out loud, Paul. You were ready to kill me because some guy called here thinking we were whoever the heck he was trying to call."

"So."

"So? That's all you've got to say? So?"

"God damn it, Dory! You need to watch your tone. Get back in here! I ain't gonna yell to you through the whole damn house. We got neighbors, you know."

She poked her head around the corner of the door frame and said, "Well, don't let them stop you. Go ahead and yell. It's what you're gonna do anyway."

"What the hell's your problem?"

She storms back into the bedroom. "MY problem? My problem is that I have a psycho husband who flips out on me about a stupid wrong number. That's insane, Paul. Nuts! Who does that?"

"I'm sorry, babe. I've been drinking a little and –"

"A little? Paul, you buy a twelve pack everyday. Everyday. And every night, when I get home, you're either passed out or as mean as a snake. And at that fishing day, Paul? The pastor had to bring him home. Do you remember that? Do you remember abandoning my son? You left my baby by himself, Paul."

"One: he wasn't by himself. The preacher was there. Two: I work hard, dammit, and I need a little something to take the edge off – "

"Edge off?! What edge? What edge are you talking about? You sit on your ass on a tow motor all day. Then when you get home, you drink til your eyeballs are floating, then when I get home after being on my feet all day, moving pallets of canned goods, and pushing carts, and lifting gallon after gallon of milk ALL DAY, you have the nerve to act like I'm just your personal sex slave. I'm sick of it, Paul."

He gets out of bed and begins hastily dressing. "Well, I'm pretty fucking sick of hearing you bitching and moaning all the time. If you're gonna do that, you should at least be putting out."

"I'm putting out right now. I'm putting YOU out." She threw his pillow at him. "You can sleep on the couch."

He dropped the pillow to the ground, clenched his fists, closed his eyes, and inhaled deeply. Dolores stepped back, anticipating a swing, but it never came.

He opened his eyes, turned to his dresser and grabbed

his keys. "Or I can go."

"Paul," she said apologetically, but there was no response. He was already in the living room, lacing up his boots. She heard a couple of footsteps toward the kitchen, followed by the jingle of keys, and then the front door slammed. Dolores sat on the edge of the bed, staring into her lap. She felt sad that the man who she thought she loved, and who she thought loved her, had turned into such a vile, hateful creature in such a short amount of time. For a fleeting moment, she felt relieved to be rid of him, but that passed quickly. Through the window she could hear Paul's truck door open, then slam shut. The engine stuttered for a second then roared to life. The gravel pinged against the underside of the truck, and the roar of the engine eventually faded into the distance. In the stillness which was left, only the crickets could be heard outside Dolores's window.

Chapter 15

Jonas sat on the roof of the abandoned doghouse in the backyard. It was a good spot to sit and think, because the maple tree which was beside it provided plenty of shade. Without consciously deciding to do so, he dangled his legs over the edge of the roof and tapped his heels against the walls, which produced a low, monotonous thud. That rhythm helped Jonas turn over ideas in his head. He really wanted to help Rev. Chambers, but he couldn't figure out exactly how. The beat suddenly stopped when Jonas thought he heard someone knocking on the front door.

He sat up straight and cocked his head toward the front of the property, and soon the knock came again. Jonas leaped from the doghouse and bounded toward the back door. He ran through the kitchen, into the living room and came to an abrupt stop at the window. He pulled back the curtain and saw Reverend Chambers on the front step, holding a bouquet of flowers and a greeting card.

Jonas opened the door. "Reverend, I was just thinking about you."

"Is that so? I've done some thinking myself since our last get-together, and I decided that I should have a talk with your momma. Is she here?"

"Nah, she's working. Why do you wanna talk to her?"

"Oh, I was going to apologize and make amends. That's

what these flowers are for. Here you go. You'll want to put those in some water soon."

"They're pretty. She'll love 'em," he said as he walked toward the kitchen. "C'mon in. I'll tell you what I was planning."

"No, I'm afraid I can't stay. And uh... as much as I hate to say it, unless your momma says it's OK, we're going to have to cancel our meetings, son."

Jonas placed the flowers on the kitchen table and hastily made his way back through the living room and into the front doorway.

"Why?" he asked with a quivering voice.

"Because it ain't right to go against your momma's wishes. It's in the Ten Commandments: Honor thy mother and father."

"But we're so close to figuring out a plan on how to get your faith back. We can't stop now."

"We have to, Jonas. I'm sorry. But maybe it'll only be temporary. Maybe together she and I can put the past behind us. It's really up to her. You be sure to give her that card for me."

"But I told you I was gonna help you," Jonas said.

The reverend smiled. "You already have, son. In more ways than you can imagine. You know, it's kind of funny that it took the faith of a child (no offense) to remind this old soul what it really means to believe. And you've helped me all you can. The rest is up to me."

Reverend Chambers leaned forward, placed his hand on Jonas' cheek, and closed his eyes. Jonas watched the old man's lips move subtly, but he couldn't hear what he was saying. Then the reverend stood upright, opened his eyes, and smiled.

"Bless you," the old man said.

Jonas threw himself toward Reverend Chambers, and he wrapped his arms around the old man's waist. Through the slobbery tears that were running down Jonas' face, he begged, "Please –"

"Go on now. Get those flowers in some water before they wilt," he said as he patted Jonas on the back.

While sniffling, Jonas reluctantly complied. He turned around and shuffled back into the house. He shut the door behind him and slumped into the recliner. Then he pulled the curtain back and watched Reverend Chambers walk away.

Chapter 16

Dolores was finishing her lunch alone at a picnic table behind the store when her phone rang. It was Paul.

"Dory, I'm going over to the house after work to get some of my things."

"What do you mean? Why?"

"Because I can't take it anymore. You're always on my case about something. If it's not one thing, it's another. And I just can't be there right now."

"You're leaving me?"

"I don't know. I just need some time to think about it all. And I can't do that there. With you."

"That's just great," she said sarcastically. "Over the phone. You couldn't even have the decency to tell me to my face?"

"I didn't want to start a fight."

"Then don't leave! We can sit down and talk it out when I get home."

"I don't even know what to say. I gotta get my head right before I can even begin talking about it. I just figured I'd call, so that you wouldn't be surprised when you saw my clothes gone. And my guitar."

"Your guitar? Your guitar?! You never even play that thing. Our marriage is falling apart, and you're concerned about an instrument you barely even know how to play?"

"Oh, good one. Make fun of my talents."

"I'm not making fun of anything, Paul. I'm trying to get you to see how crazy this all is. You're going to leave because I didn't have sex with you last night?"

"No, it's more than that."

"Then at least give me the opportunity to hear you out. That's all I'm asking for. Just for you to talk to me face to face, and tell me."

There was silence on the other end of the line, which was eventually broken by a long sigh. "Fine. I'll see you when you get home. But my night shift starts tonight."

"Thank you, Paul. I'll try to get home before you have to leave for work."

Dolores' phone beeped, indicating that the call had ended. Paul had hung up.

She took a drink from her soda and started to close the phone, but she stopped. Under Paul's name, on the incoming call list, she saw the call from the wrong number. She swallowed the soda with a gulp, closed her phone and tossed it into her purse.

"Jackass," she said to herself before throwing her wrinkled, brown paper bag into the trash can near the door.

Chapter 17

Later that evening, Jonas was watching cartoons on TV
when he heard Paul's truck pull up in front of the house. He
jumped up from the couch, turned the TV off and ran to his
room, hoping Paul wouldn't notice he was there. To the
benefit of Jonas, it worked. Paul opened the front door,
walked directly to the bedroom and began stuffing his
clothes into an old, tattered duffle bag. After a few shirts and
a couple pairs of jeans, he threw in a couple pairs of socks,
some clean underwear, and his aftershave. He carried the bag
to the kitchen, where he took the remaining three cans of
beer. After he shut the fridge door and zipped up the duffle
bag, Paul turned around to leave, and he noticed the flowers
on the table from Reverend Chambers. He picked up the
heavy envelope with the greeting card in it. It only read,
"Dolores" on the front. He knew he didn't buy it for her.

"That goddam whore," was all Paul said as he threw the
card down on the table and stormed out of the house. He
pulled out of the drive and headed toward the bar for a quick
one before going to the factory to begin his shift.

Jonas listened closely to the door to be sure Paul had
left before he opened the bedroom door. He walked to the
living room, turned the TV back on, and flopped onto the
couch. The images on the screen and the noise from the
speakers were just background static to Jonas, however. His
mind was occupied with the conversation he had with the

reverend. He didn't understand what the old man meant when he said Jonas had already helped him. They hadn't even come up with a solid plan, really. To Jonas, the reverend seemed different somehow. He couldn't quite figure it out, but in some way, the old man seemed almost hopeful, and that gave Jonas some relief. But not so much as to overcome the pain of the news that he may no longer be able to see him, talk to him, or spend time with him. It all depended on whether Dolores would give him permission, and he didn't expect his mother to be receptive to the idea at all. Jonas spent the next two hours lying on his back on the couch, with his head turned toward the TV, staring at the flickering images which started to cast a bluish glow onto the walls as evening turned to night.

Jonas had been lying on the couch in a daze for so long that he was startled when he heard Dolores speaking to him. She was standing at the end of the couch, her smock draped over her purse in her left hand, and her car keys still in her right hand.

"Jonas, where's Paul?"

Jonas pulled himself up by the back of the couch and rubbed his eyes.

"Was Paul here, Jonas?" she asked as she turned off the TV.

He cleared his throat. "Yeah, I went to my room when he came home. But he went to the bedroom and rustled around in there, then went to the kitchen, messed around in there, then he said something and left. I couldn't make out what he said."

"Oh," Dolores said, disappointed. She dropped her purse, smock, and keys onto the coffee table, sat in the recliner and began taking off her shoes. She briefly thought about telling Jonas that Paul might not be living there anymore. But she quickly changed her mind. "He's your son, not your shrink," she thought to herself, and decided to wait.

With her toes, Dolores nudged her shoes under the coffee table. She let out a long sigh and pulled the lever on the side of the chair. The footrest swung out with a loud, metallic clang, and the chair back made a clicking, clinking noise as it lowered. She turned toward Jonas and asked, "Could you get a cold pop from the fridge for your tired momma, honey?"

Jonas groaned.

"C'mon, I just got home. My feet are sore. Please?"

"Okay," Jonas said as he got up from the couch and stretched, "but I want to talk to you about something." He shuffled toward the kitchen, and returned with a can of pop and the card from the old man.

Dolores took the can and eyed the card. "What's that?"

"It's from Reverend Chambers. He came by to give you that and the flowers."

She closed the recliner and stood up. "What flowers?"

"Here in the kitchen. He said I should put 'em in water,

but I don't know how to do that, so I figured I'd wait for you to come home."

"I don't know what he's up to, but if he thinks –" she said as she walked toward the kitchen.

"Momma, he's trying to apologize. Open the card."

She picked up the bouquet and examined it suspiciously. Then she returned it to the table and tore open the envelope. Inside the envelope was a greeting card, and on the front was a picture of a butterfly resting on a daisy. She opened the card to find that it was blank, but the reverend had enclosed a neatly folded letter which was written on personal stationery.

She unfolded it and began reading aloud, "Dolores, I know you distrust me, and probably rightly so, but I felt that I needed to talk to you. Please understand that I had the best of intentions when I got involved in that fiasco. I really only wanted to help everyone, and I got swindled by that con man as much as everyone else. I lost a large portion of our savings in that mess. Worst of all, I lost my beloved wife. But what I've learned since then, and largely in part to your son, is that we're all only humans after all. We make mistakes sometimes, even when we're trying to do what is right. And what separates us from the evil in this world is not whether we do wrong, it's whether we're able to admit our faults and seek forgiveness from those we've wronged. I have lived with the burden of guilt weighing on me every day since, and now I'm trying to be at peace with myself, and my Maker, and hopefully, with you. Please accept my most heartfelt apologies. Unfortunately, they're all I can give you. Sincerely, Rev. James Chambers II."

She folded the letter and returned it, and the card, to the envelope. She didn't know what to think. First, Paul leaves her, and then the old man was trying to apologize. All of this added to the aching in her feet and her head. She was completely spent from her long shift, and her tired mind was trying uselessly to process the day's events using information gathered from her exhausted emotions. She just wanted to go to bed.

"So?" Jonas asked softly.

She blinked back the tears which were forming in the corners of her eyes. "Let me sleep on it, Jonas. I just have to get some rest. I have to go in to work early tomorrow, so if you're not up when I leave, you're going to have to fix yourself breakfast. You need to brush your teeth and hit the hay, too," she said as she kissed the top of his head and walked to her bedroom.

Jonas stood up, but he had been reclined for so long that the rapid ascent made him dizzy. He wobbled in front of the couch for a few seconds before regaining his balance and retiring to his bedroom.

Chapter 18

West of Dorn's Hill was a smaller, unnamed hill. From just the right spot along the side of the road on County Road 30, a clearing between the trees would allow a glimpse of both hills aligned perfectly; the unnamed hill in front, and Dorn's Hill in back, with the peaks centered exactly. The small hill looked like a shorter, shaved version of its densely wooded, massive sister. Most of the western exposure of the smaller hill, including the crest, was taken up by a sheep pasture. Jonas had been to the pasture on a field trip when he was in the third grade, but he had mostly forgotten about it. But as he slept, Jonas was dreaming about that pasture.

He was standing near the bald summit, looking west, over the empty field. Beyond the pasture, he saw a thick row of trees along the road, and beyond the road were more tree-covered hills. It was cold, and the skies were overcast, which dulled the colors of the trees and grass, and gave Jonas the impression that he was in a black and white photo. Jonas squinted into the strong and steady wind, and he watched it roll the low, dark clouds toward him. It seemed to him as if he was watching the scene in fast forward, as an endless stream of churning, gray clouds rushed toward him.

In the distance, nearly as far as Jonas could see, he spotted a lighter colored patch of clouds come over the horizon. The small patch of clouds began to brighten, and it continued to rush toward him. Soon the clouds parted, and a beam of sunlight shot out. It not only illuminated every leaf on every tree in its path, but Jonas could also see the bold, bright colors of everything it touched, while everything outside the beam's footprint remained dark shades of gray.

When the shaft of light finally reached Jonas, everything stopped. The clouds were motionless, and the wind had gone still. He stood in the center of the circle of light which the beam had cast all around him. Then he closed his eyes and raised his head toward the bright, yellow glow. To Jonas, it felt like an all-encompassing warmth. It felt a lot like when he used to hug his grandmother.

Suddenly, Jonas heard the old man's voice calling his name. He shielded his eyes from the light and looked across the pasture to see Reverend Chambers at the far end, calling to him.

"Jonas! Get up. I'm running late," shouted Dolores as she tossed open his bedroom door, rousing Jonas from his dream. He groaned and turned over to face the window, and she continued to the bathroom to get a hair brush.

"Jonas, baby, you're gonna have to make yourself a bowl of cereal, hon. I'm leaving. Get up!" She repeated from the hallway while violently brushing her hair back. She hurried into the living room, shoved her feet into her work shoes, and quickly returned to Jonas' room.

She leaned over the bed and kissed him quickly on the back of the head. "Get up, Jonas! Get you something to eat.

I'll be home earlier tonight than last night. Promise."

Knowing that she wouldn't leave until he showed some signs of life, he waved.

"Love you, honey," she said, and jogged to the living room. With a bow and a swipe, she gathered her purse and smock from the coffee table. She swung the door open and spun around. "Call me if it's an emergency!" she shouted before closing the front door.

Jonas pulled the thin, cotton sheet over his face and tried to go back to sleep, but he couldn't. He wanted to return to the pasture from his dream. The sunlight felt like warm, soft towels, fresh from the dryer, just like when he helped his mother fold laundry. He opened his eyes and saw only shades of bright, but hazy, yellow as the morning sun shined through the thin clouds and onto the sheet. It was a barely adequate substitute for the sunlight from his dream, but still beautiful nonetheless. He eventually came to terms with having to get up, and he sighed as he pushed the sheet toward his waist and sat up to stretch. He yawned heartily, and when he did, his stomach growled and moaned, which reminded him of what Dolores had said to him before she left.

He shuffled into the kitchen, wearing only his underwear, and one sock. He pulled open the fridge door and removed the milk and sat it on the table. From the cabinet next to the fridge, he pulled out a box of corn flakes and sat it on the table next to the milk. With a bowl from the drying rack and spoon from the drawer, his breakfast was ready. He plopped down onto the chair and poured the flakes into the bowl and added milk. As he ate, only the sounds of crunching corn flakes and a clinking spoon could be heard. Clink, slurp, crunch, crunch, crunch, was the rhythm, and it continued until Jonas propped up his tired face with his left hand. That was when he noticed it. Or didn't notice it, rather. The calcified lump of bone which normally protruded from his jawline was gone.

He nearly choked on a mouthful of corn flakes, then spat them into the bowl as he darted from the table to the bathroom mirror. There he saw what his hand first felt: a smooth, normal jawline. He gasped and turned his head left, then right, then back left again to compare the two sides. His heart was pounding, and he didn't know if he was going to cry, or laugh, or both. His first thought was to go tell the old man about the miracle, but his body was a step ahead of him, and he found himself about to run out the front door without wearing any clothes.

"Shoot!" he said between his teeth as he turned around and ran toward the bedroom to hastily throw on some clothes. He returned to the living room and bolted through the doorway to the outside. He hopped onto his bike, pointed it toward the reverend's house, and didn't stop peddling.

Chapter 19

Paul knew a place on the outskirts of town where he and his buddies would build bonfires and ride ATVs. It was secluded, accessed only by a dirt road just off the state route, on the east side of town. After he finished his shift, he drove there to get some fresh air and think. In his lap was an open beer can, and in the seat next to him were eleven more, which were all about to be opened soon. There were two more in the duffle bag in the bed of the truck, but they were for later, after he figured out where he was going to sleep. He was still angry about the flowers, and he was considering confronting her, but he didn't trust his temper when they fought. He thought it was best to just stay away. A small, quiet meadow, surrounded by sparse stands of pine and maple, was the perfect place for him to park and think of a way to find Dolores's "other man".

Paul finished off the first beer, crushed the can, and tossed it through the sliding rear window into the bed of the truck. He cracked open another, and turned on the radio. The sound of steel guitars and electric fiddles filled the dense, moist morning air. By his sixth beer, he had a half-assed plan, and by his ninth, he had forgotten his original plan and concocted an even more absurd and certain-to-fail plan. Having never bothered to open the card, he had no idea who gave her the flowers. If he were to go back to the house, he could find the card, figure out who he was, then look him up in the phone book and settle this business "like a man". He tossed the tenth can into the bed of the truck, let out a belch, and turned the key in the ignition. The thick morning air could no longer hold in its moisture, and it began drizzling as Paul pulled onto the black top and accelerated toward town.

His mind was a haze except for the plan, and even the finer details of the plan were beginning to cloud over. As he drove, Paul swerved violently as he tried to rehearse a few lines of what he would say when he met the other guy, but by the time he passed the city limits sign, it was all becoming unintelligible.

The drizzle had turned to rain as he sped through the first intersection downtown, just as the traffic light turned from yellow to red. As he approached the second intersection, something up ahead caught his eye. He blinked and opened his eyes wide in order to get them to uncross, and he saw Jonas riding his bike in the same direction toward Carlisle Street. He was pedaling furiously, and was soaking wet from rain. Paul turned his head in Jonas' direction as he passed, and quickly realized he was about to miss his turn. He yanked the steering wheel to the right, and the back tires lost traction and slid to the left. Paul over-corrected and began skidding right. The tires passed over a dry spot on the pavement underneath the branches of a maple tree, and they regained their grip. But the sideways motion of the truck had too much momentum, and the truck flipped over in the street.

The sound of breaking glass and scraping metal echoed against the houses along Carlisle Street as the truck rolled onto its side then roof. It came to rest on the sidewalk, with the cab on the concrete and the mangled bed against a tree near the curb.

Jonas rounded the corner, and stopped short of running into a growing crowd of onlookers. He recognized Paul's truck. A number of people rushed to the truck. One man was helping Paul exit the cab through the space left by the shattered window, and a small group of others were trying to push the bed of the truck away from the tree. When Paul was free from the truck, the group all pushed at once, and the truck plowed a deep gouge into the grass in front of the tree.

Jonas stretched to get a view from between the jostling elbows and shoulders of the bystanders. He managed to catch a glimpse of the scene, and his stomach jumped into his throat. He had never before seen so much blood. Paul was scraped and still coherent enough to curse at those who had come to rescue him, but he didn't appear seriously injured. Jonas looked around at the group of bystanders to see if the reverend had heard the commotion and had come out of his house, which was two doors down from where Paul's truck came to rest. But the old man was not in the crowd. Jonas pushed his way through the crowd and toward Paul. When he cleared the forest of grown-ups, he saw the old man lying on the ground, between the truck and the tree against which he had been pinned.

"Reverend!" he shouted, and ran toward the old man.

"Stay back, kid. You don't want to see that," said an onlooker as he grabbed Jonas by the arm, pulling him away from the horrific scene.

Jonas twisted free from the man, who had managed to pull him back toward his bicycle.

"Listen, kid, somebody got hurt bad. It's not something you should be seeing," said the man.

"That's my friend!" he shouted and ran back through the crowd, losing the do-gooder in the bustle. But when he got toward the front of the crowd, a police officer was herding the crowd away from the scene while EMTs worked on Paul.

"That's my friend! Why aren't you helping him?" he shouted at the officer.

"Everybody back, please. We need you to move back. If you saw what happened, I'll be taking your statements, but I need everyone to just back up," said the cop.

Jonas looked at Paul and the EMT, then looked at the reverend, who was being covered with a sheet by another EMT. It became clear to Jonas, and realizing there was nothing he could do, he cried as he walked back toward his bike.

Jonas thought about the reverend, and how he would never get a chance to witness the miracle he had performed. In the chaos of the accident, Jonas had almost forgotten about the miracle. He placed his hand on his face to remind himself, but the lump was there. Earlier, he was certain it was gone. He had seen it in the mirror. There was no lump, yet at that corner, in the rain, Jonas felt a lump along the left side of his jaw. He walked up to the window of the building on the corner and looked closely at his reflection. The growth had returned as surely as it had gone earlier.

"It doesn't mean it didn't happen," he said to himself.

Jonas grabbed the handlebars of his bike and righted it. He hiked one leg over the seat, and placed his foot on the high pedal. He gave one last look toward the scene of the crash, then stood on the pedal and began rolling toward home.

THE END

12227543R00074

Made in the USA
Charleston, SC
21 April 2012